I0764712

FUN
WITH
MATHS

By the same author

Little Red Book Series

Little Red Book of Slang-Chat Room Slang

Little Red Book of English Vocabulary Today

Little Red Book of Grammar Made Easy

Little Red Book of English Proverbs

Little Red Book of Prepositions

Little Red Book of Idioms and Phrases

Little Red Book of Euphemisms

Little Red Book of Effective Speaking Skills

Little Red Book of Modern Writing Skills

Little Red Book of Verbal Phrases

Little Red Book of Synonyms

Little Red Book of Antonyms

Little Red Book of Common Errors

Little Red Book of Letter Writing

Little Red Book of Perfect Written English

Little Red Book of Essay Writing

Little Red Book of Word Power

Little Red Book of Spelling

Little Red Book of Language Checklist

Little Red Book of Word Fact

Little Red Book: A Child's First Dictionary

A2Z Book Series

A2Z Quiz Book

A2Z Book of Word Origins

Others

The Book of Fun Facts

The Book of More Fun Facts

The Book of Firsts and Lasts

The Book of Virtues

The Book of Motivation

Read Write Right: Common Errors in English

The Students' Companion

Fun with Puzzles

Fun with Numbers

Fun with Riddles

TERRY O'BRIEN

RUPA

Published by
Rupa Publications India Pvt. Ltd 2013
7/16, Ansari Road, Daryaganj
New Delhi 110002

Sales centres:

Allahabad Bengaluru Chennai
Hyderabad Jaipur Kathmandu
Kolkata Mumbai

ISBN: 978-81-291-2382-4

10 9 8 7 6 5 4 3 2 1

Typeset in Times New Roman 10/12
by Innovative Processors, New Delhi

Acknowledgement

A special thanks to Allen O'Brien, my son,
who assisted me in having fun while
compiling and re-imagining what's
essential for such a book

Introduction

There are so many fun and easy activities you can do to help form your child's development of early math concepts - and most of these can also provide important early learning experiences.

Life would be much easier if you could easily estimate:

- How much a bill would be
- Which product was the best value for money
- Lengths and angles

Also, wouldn't it be good if you could quickly guess how many people were in a room, how many cars in the street, how many boxes on the shelf, or even how many seagulls on the beach?

We are not talking exact answers here, but answers that are good enough for your life.

This isn't just a collection of silly tricks, like, 'Take a number, multiply it by nine, add your age, divide by the number of socks in your sock drawer, subtract your grandmother's birthday, and I'll tell you some meaningless number that will bore you to tears.' This book is different.

Here is a book that provides you with fun mathematics. Fun does not necessarily mean easy. As a subject anything that becomes challenging is fun maths for all.

Follow The Format

Sequences and patterns such as 3, 6, 9, 12, 15, 18. . . or 30, 40, 50, 60, 70, 80 . . . are very much a part of day-to-day mathematics. All you need to do is remember them and get into the habit of using them every now and then. And do that in such a way that 30, 40, 50, 60. . . can be adapted to 33, 43, 53, 63, 73. . .

Practice Makes You Perfect

What makes mathematics different from other subjects is the speed with which one can solve those numerical problems. Of course, you first need to learn new skills and practice them. As you practice, you get faster and the task gets easier. And thus, speed is taken care of!

Think Like The Tortoise and The Hare

The Hare way of thinking:

- ✓ This one likes to work with formulas and set methods.
- ✓ This one works step by step, preferring to write things down.
- ✓ This one sees the details.
- ✓ They see numbers exactly as they are written — a sort of numerical equivalent of a literal interpretation.

Check this out:

340
+97
437

This one will add 340 and 97 step by step, starting with

the units—that is 0, add 7, then 4 add 9 and finally 3. Add (the carried) 1 to give an answer of 437.

The Tortoise way of thinking:

✓ This one goes straight to an answer.
✓ This one rarely writes down while working out.
✓ This one likes to see the whole picture — they overview.
✓ This one is intuitive and can be confused by formulas.
✓ This one sees a broad value in numbers, replacing them with convenient values. For them, 57 is 3 digits less than 60.

Check this out:

340
+97
437

This one will look at 97 and round it up to 100, add 340 and 100 and subtract 3 (which made 97 into 100), getting an answer of 437, without writing anything down.

NOTE: It is best if you can learn how to make use of both thinking styles.

The moral of the story:

In order to be versatile in mental maths, you should draw on both styles of thinking.

Take Risks to Master Math

Also, never give up before you even try. No wonder Mathophobia is the most dreadful phobia amongst students. Remember, good mental maths is all about taking risks. If you look at every numberological equation and say: 'I don't know where to start', then you will never really start... and never really learn. So make sure you practice and experiment with new ideas.

Addition

Go from left to right

If the usual norm is anything to go by, we normally start adding numbers from right to left. When doing mental maths, make sure you start from the left.

Check this out:

45
+32

If you start from the left this is how you will go about it: 45 + 30 + 2, since the first sum changes only the left-most digit. This sum is easier to do in our heads: 45 + 30 = 75, and 75 + 2 = 77.
Try to visualise the numbers, and avoid repeating unnecessary information in your head . Try to see 45, 75, 77.

Addition of two digits without carrying forth

To make sure the two-digit addition problems are a cakewalk, you've got to make sure that you do not *carry* any numbers forward. And how does one do this? Make sure the sum of the first digit equals 9 or below. The same rule shall apply to the second digit as well.
Check this out:

47
+ 32 (30 +2)

Now, to add 47 + 32, first add 30. Later add the 2. After

adding 30, the problem becomes much simpler. In this case it is 77 + 2, which is equal to 79.

Check this out:

47+32 = 77 (+2) = 79

Addition of two digits with carry forth

67
+28 (20+8)

Making sure you add from left to right, you can simplify the problem by adding 67 + 20 = 87 and then to 87 you add the 8 so that the total equals 95.

67+28 = 87+8 = 95

Check this out:

84
+ 57 (50+7)

First add 84 + 50 = 134 and then add 134+7=141. In other words,

84+57 = 134+7 = 141

Also, check this out:

68
+ 45 (40+5)

First add 68 + 40 = 108, and then to 108 add 5, which is equal to 113!

And finally, check this out:

80
+ 75 (70+5)

First add 80 + 70 = 150, and then to 150 add 5, which is

equal to 155.

Addition of three-digits to four-digit numbers

(*Where the non-zero digits overlap in one place*)

2700
+ 567

2700+ 500 = 3200. To this add 67 and the result is 3267.

Check this out:

3240	**3240**
+18	**+72**

40 + 18 = 58 and to this add 3200. The result is 3258.
40 + 72 is more than 100, so the answer will be 3300 something . Which means 40 +72 = 112, and thus the answer is 3312.

(*Where the non-zero digits overlap in two places*)

4560
+ 171 (100+ 71)
4560 + 171 = 4660 + 71 = 4731 +100 +71

Addition of unequal digits

415
+1932

Just remember, it's easier to think of 1932 + 415 (add the smaller number to the bigger one).

Now, 1932 + 400 + 10 + 5 = 2332 + 10 + 5 (we added 4 to 19) = 2342 + 5 (we added 1 to 3) = 2347 (we added 5 to 2).

Addition of large digits like 7, 8, 9

If you want to add 9 to a number, you can just add 10 and

then subtract 1. Similarly, if you want to add 8, you can add 10 and then subtract 2. This can be particularly helpful when we are adding numbers ending with a large digit, such as 7, 8, or 9.

For instance,

43
+8
43 + (8+2) 10 = 53 -2 = 51

First adding 10 and then subtracting 2 makes the sum easier to work out mentally.

So here goes the formula:

a+ b = (a + 1) 0 = 10 × (a + 1), and then subtract 10 and then subtract it with b.

413
+28
413 + 30 – minus 2 = 441

Check Your Answer Too!

Check your answer with the module 9 formula

Did you know. . .

If you divide an integer 'x' by 9, the remainder obtained is the same as the sum of the digits of 'x', module 9.

Check this out:

x = 67

Since 67 = 9 × 7 + 4, the remainder is 4. Now 6 + 7 = 13 and equiv 4 (mod 9).

Casting out nines to check addition is simply the process of checking if the remainder module 9 of the numbers in the sum add up to the remainder module 9 of our answer.

Check this out:

8243 (8)
+ 3434 (5)
11677 (4)

The numbers in the bracket represent the remainders mod 9. 8 + 5 and equiv 4 (mod 9). So we have some evidence that our answer is correct.

Be doubly sure:

Casting out nines is not a proof that our answer is correct. However, it is a method to determine if the answer is wrong: If the sum of remainders doesn't add up to the remainder of our answer, we know for sure we made a mistake somewhere.

Check this out:

413
+831
+28

The sum of the remainders mod 9 is 8 + 3 + 1 and equiv 3 (mod 9). So if we obtained, say, 1322 & equiv 8 (mod 9), we can be certain that we made a mistake.

Want to Tip That Waiter?

We often end up wondering how much is too much when it comes to tipping the waiter in a restaurant. Well, it involves a simple mental math application.

Here is what you need to do:

Suppose your bill at a restaurant came to ₹420, and you wanted to leave a 15% tip.

✓ First we calculate 10% of 420, which is ₹42.

✓ Cut that number in half, we get ₹21. This is 5% of the bill.

✓ Adding these numbers together gives us ₹63, which is exactly 15% of the bill.

And this is how you can calculate your shopping festival discounts and special offers!

Now check this out:

If you need to leave a 15% tip, here is the easy way to do it. Work out 10% (divide the number by 10) – then add that number to half its value and you have your answer:

15% of ₹25 = (10% of 25) + ((10% of 25) / 2)

₹2.50 + ₹1.25 = ₹3.75

Get Your Basics Right

0+ 0 = 0. 10+ 10 = 20... so on and so forth

This is the core of all additions and subtractions. So if you know that 3 + 8 = 11, you will end up using this each and every time an 8 is added to 3.

Check this out:

3 + 8 = 11

3 + 18 = 21

13 + 8 = 21

13 + 28 = 41

23 + 18 = 41

300 + 800 = 1100

30 + 80 = 110

The idea is pretty clear. One basic fact can be used as a knowledge tool for various other examples and mental math problems as well!

How To Write A Cheque

The best way to write a cheque is to make the following diagram in your mind. This is called the Place Value Grid.

Check this out:

Million	Hundred thousand	Ten thousand	Thousand	Hundred	Ten	Unit

This is the best way that will help you fill up your blank cheque bang on!

A cheque of nine million, six thousand and ten:

1. Place the nine of the million in the million box:

Million	Hundred thousand	Ten thousand	Thousand	Hundred	Ten	Unit
9						

2. Place the six of the thousand in the thousand box:

Million	Hundred thousand	Ten thousand	Thousand	Hundred	Ten	Unit
9			6			

3. For the ten, first place the one in the ten box:

Million	Hundred thousand	Ten thousand	Thousand	Hundred	Ten	Unit
9			6		1	

4. Now place the zero in the unit box:

Million	Hundred thousand	Ten thousand	Thousand	Hundred	Ten	Unit
9			6		1	0

Which means a cheque of nine million, six thousand and ten in words reads as 9 00 6 010! Here is how:

Million	Hundred thousand	Ten thousand	Thousand	Hundred	Ten	Unit
9	0	0	6	0	1	0

Know Your Thousands

The number of DIGITS in a number gives an idea of the value of the number. In other words, the first (and lowest) five-figure number is 10000 and the last (and biggest) is 99 999.

Similarly, the first six-figure number is 100 000 and the last is 999 99 (one short of a million).

And just to help you remember your thousands, here is more.

Check this out:

✓ Hundreds = three-figure numbers.
✓ Thousands = four-figure numbers.
✓ Ten thousands = five-figure numbers.
✓ Hundred thousands = six-figure numbers.
✓ Millions = seven-figure numbers.
✓ Billions = ten-figure numbers.
✓ Trillions = thirteen-figure numbers.

Binary Addition

101
+101

Step 1:

To add these two numbers, we first consider the 'ones' column and calculate 1 + 1, which (in binary) results in 10. We 'carry' the 1 to the 'tens' column, and leave the 0 in the 'ones' column.

Step 2:

Moving on to the 'tens' column, we calculate 1 + (0 + 0), which gives 1. Nothing 'carries' to the 'hundreds' column, and we leave the 1 in the 'tens' column.

Step 3:

Moving on to the 'hundreds' column, we calculate 1 + 1, which gives 10. We 'carry' the 1 to the 'thousands' column, leaving the 0 in the 'hundreds' column.

101
+101
1010

Check this one out too:

$$\begin{array}{r} \mathbf{1011} \\ \mathbf{+1011} \\ \mathbf{10110} \end{array}$$

Note that in the 'tens' column, we have 1 + (1 + 1), where the first 1 is 'carried' from the 'ones' column. Recall that in binary,

$$\begin{aligned} \mathbf{1 + 1 + 1} &= \mathbf{10 + 1} \\ &= \mathbf{11} \end{aligned}$$

Break Time

Pick A Number

Pick a number between 2 and 9

Example: 7

Multiply this number by 2

Example: 7 x 2 = 14

Add 5

Example: 14 + 5 = 19

Multiply this number by 50

Example: 19 x 50 = 950

If you already had your birthday this year, add 1761

Example: 950 + 1761 = 2711

If you have not yet celebrated your birthday this year, add 1760.

Example: 950 + 1760 = 2710

Subtract your year of birth

Example: 2711 - 1987 = 724

Magic:

The first number is the number you picked and the last two numbers are your age.

Birthday math

Find a calculator or a pencil and paper.

Ask your friend or eveyone to write down their birthday.

Example: September 28, 1986

Ask your friend (or everyone in the room) to write down the number of the month he/she/they were born.

Example: 9 (born in September)

Multiply the month by 4

9 x 4 = 36

Add 13

36 + 13 = 49

Multiply by 25

49 x 25 = 1225

Subtract 200

1225 - 200 = 1025

Add the day of the month he/she/they were born

1025 + 28 = 1053

Multiply by 2

1053 x 2 = 2106

Subtract 40

2106 – 40 = 2066

Multiply by 50

2066 x 50 = 103300

Add the last two digits of your year of birth (1986)

103300 + 86 = 103386

Ask your friend to give you their result

103386

Now you can magically tell them their birth date.

Here's how to do it:

Subtract 10500 from their result

103386 - 10500 = 92886

9 = month of September

28 = day of birth

86 = year of birth

Sequence in Math

A Sequence is a group of numbers placed in a particular order.

Types of Sequences

Arithmetic Sequence

What is it? The difference between one digit and the next is a constant. Which in other words means, you just add some value each time ... till infinity.

Sequence:

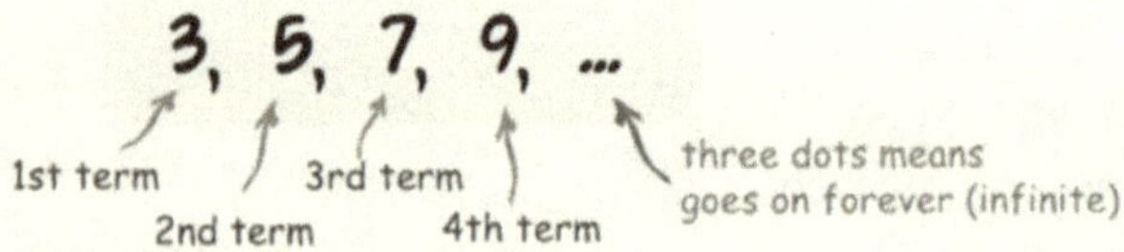

("term", "element" or "member" mean the same thing)

Example:

1, 4, 7, 10, 13, 16, 19, 22, 25, ...

This sequence has a difference of 3 between each number.

$$x_n = 3n-2$$

In general, you could write an arithmetic sequence like this:

$$\{a, a+d, a+2d, a+3d, ... \}$$

where:

- **a** is the first term, and
- **d** is the difference between the terms (called the **'common difference'**)

And you can make the rule by:

$$x_n = a + d\,(n-1)$$

(*We use 'n-1' because **d** is not used in the 1st term*).

Geometric Sequences

What is it? Here each term is found by multiplying the previous term by a constant.

Example:

2, 4, 8, 16, 32, 64, 128, 256, ...

This sequence has a factor of 2 between each number. Rule is $x_n = 2^n$

In general, you could write a geometric sequence like this:

$$\{a, ar, ar^2, ar^3, ... \}$$

where:

- a is the first term, and
- r is the factor between the terms (called the 'common ratio')

r should not be 0.

- When **r=0**, you get the sequence (a,0,0,...) which is not geometric

And the rule is:

$$x_n = ar^{(n-1)}$$

Triangular Numbers

What is it? This is generated from a pattern of dots, which form a triangle. By adding another row of dots and counting all the dots we can find the next number of the sequence:

1, 3, 6, 10, 15, 21, 28, 36, 45, ...

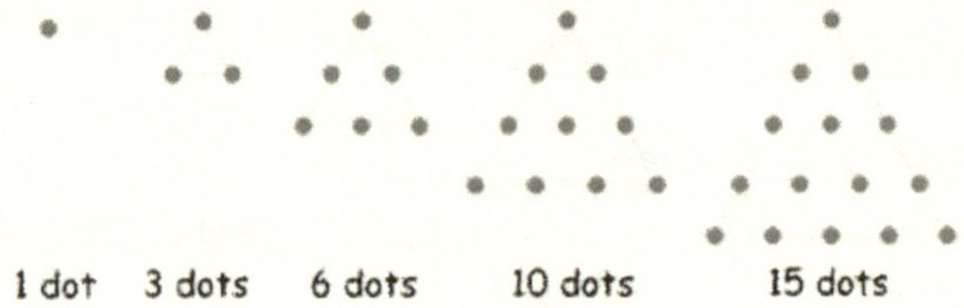

1 dot 3 dots 6 dots 10 dots 15 dots

But it is easier to use this Rule:

$$x_n = n(n+1)/2$$

Example:

- the 5th Triangular Number is $x_5 = 5(5+1)/2 = \mathbf{15}$,
- and the sixth is $x_6 = 6(6+1)/2 = \mathbf{21}$

Square Numbers

1, 4, 9, 16, 25, 36, 49, 64, 81, ...

The next number is made by squaring where it is in the pattern.

$$\mathbf{x_n = n^2}$$

Cube Numbers

$$1, 8, 27, 64, 125, 216, 343, 512, 729, ...$$

The next number is made by cubing where it is in the pattern.

$$x_n = n^3$$

Fibonacci Sequence

$$0, 1, 1, 2, 3, 5, 8, 13, 21, 34, ...$$

The next number is found by adding the two numbers before it together:

- The 2 is found by adding the two numbers before it (1+1)
- The 21 is found by adding the two numbers before it (8+13)

$$x_n = x_{n-1} + x_{n-2}$$

That rule is interesting because it depends on the values of the previous two terms.

The Fibonacci Sequence is numbered from 0 onwards like this:

$n=$	0	1	2	3	4	5	6	7	8	9	10	11	12	13	14 ...
$x_n=$	0	1	1	2	3	5	8	13	21	34	55	89	144	233	377 ...

Example: term '6' would be calculated like this:

$$x_6 = x_{6-1} + x_{6-2} = x_5 + x_4 = 5 + 3 = 8$$

The 24 Hour Clock decoded

Normally the time is shown as Hours:Minutes. There are 24 Hours in a Day and 60 Minutes in each Hour.

Example: 10:25 means 10 Hours and 25 Minutes

There are two major ways to show the time: '24 Hour Clock' or 'AM/PM'.

- With the **24 Hour Clock** the time is shown as how many hours and minutes since midnight.
- With **AM/PM** (or '12 Hour Clock') the day is split into the 12 Hours running from Midnight to Noon (the AM hours) and the other 12 Hours running from Noon to Midnight (the PM hours).

AM	**PM**
Ante Meridiem*	Post Meridiem*
Latin for 'before midday'	*Latin for 'after midday'*

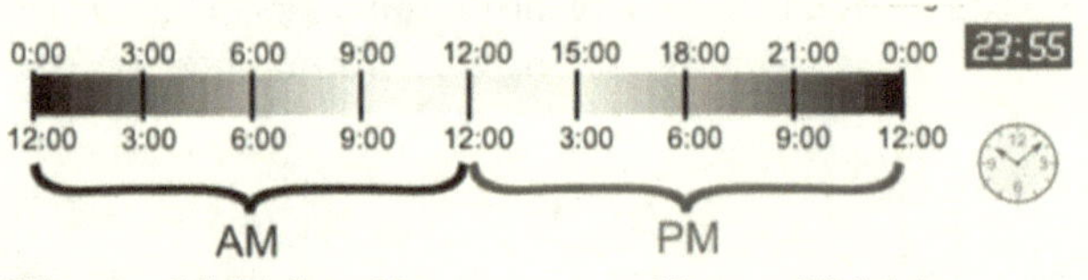

When:	Midnight to Noon	Noon to Midnight
24 Hour Clock:	0:00 to 11:59	12:00 to 23:59

Converting AM/PM to 24 Hour Clock

For the first hour of the day (12 Midnight to 12:59 AM), subtract 12 Hours

Examples: 12 Midnight = 0:00, 12:35 AM = 0:35

From 1:00 AM to 12:59 PM, no change

Examples: 11:20 AM = 11:20, 12:30 PM = 12:30

From 1:00 PM to 11:59 PM, add 12 Hours

Example: 4:45 PM = 16:45, 11:50 PM = 23:50

Converting 24 Hour Clock to AM/PM

For the first hour of the day (0:00 to 0:59), add 12 Hours, make it 'AM'

Example: 0:10 = 12:10 AM, 0:40 = 12:40 AM

From 1:00 to 11:59, just make it 'AM'

Example: 1:15 = 1:15 AM, 11:25 = 11:25 AM

From 12:00 to 12:59, just make it 'PM'

Example: 12:10 = 12:10 PM, 12:55 = 12:55 PM

From 13:00 to 23:59, subtract 12 Hours, make it 'PM'

Example: 14:55 = 2:55 PM, 23:30 = 11:30 PM

Here is a side-by-side comparison of the 24 Hour Clock and AM/PM:

Example: on the hour		Example: 10 minutes past	
24 Hour Clock	**AM / PM**	**24 Hour Clock**	**AM / PM**
0:00	12 Midnight	0:10	12:10 AM
1:00	1:00 AM	1:10	1:10 AM
2:00	2:00 AM	2:10	2:10 AM
3:00	3:00 AM	3:10	3:10 AM
4:00	4:00 AM	4:10	4:10 AM
5:00	5:00 AM	5:10	5:10 AM
6:00	6:00 AM	6:10	6:10 AM
7:00	7:00 AM	7:10	7:10 AM
8:00	8:00 AM	8:10	8:10 AM
9:00	9:00 AM	9:10	9:10 AM
10:00	10:00 AM	10:10	10:10 AM
11:00	11:00 AM	11:10	11:10 AM
12:00	12 Noon	12:10	12:10 PM
13:00	1:00 PM	13:10	1:10 PM
14:00	2:00 PM	14:10	2:10 PM
15:00	3:00 PM	15:10	3:10 PM
16:00	4:00 PM	16:10	4:10 PM

(*Contd*)

17:00	5:00 PM	17:10	5:10 PM
18:00	6:00 PM	18:10	6:10 PM
19:00	7:00 PM	19:10	7:10 PM
20:00	8:00 PM	20:10	8:10 PM
21:00	9:00 PM	21:10	9:10 PM
22:00	10:00 PM	22:10	10:10 PM
23:00	11:00 PM	23:10	11:10 PM

Midnight and Noon

'12 AM' and '12 PM' can cause confusion, so we prefer '12 Midnight' and '12 Noon'.

Midnight has another problem - there is nothing to tell you 'is this the beginning or ending of the day'.

Suppose you are leaving for Japan at 'midnight' on 12th March, what day should you say goodbye? Do you get there on the 12th (assuming you leave at the very start of the 11th), or the 12th (assuming you leave at the end of the 11th)?

It is better to use:

- 11:59 PM or 12:01 AM, or
- 23:59 or 0:01 (24 Hour Clock)

which the railroads, airlines and military actually do.

So, if you see something like 'offer ends midnight October 15th' make sure to use one minute before or after so there is no confusion!

Squares and Square Roots

To square a number, just multiply it by itself...

Example: What is 3 squared?

3 Squared = 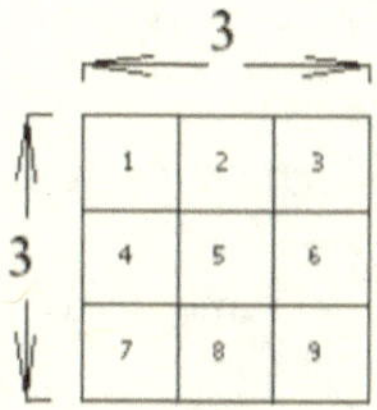

$= 3 \times 3 = \mathbf{9}$

'Squared' is often written as a little 2 like this:

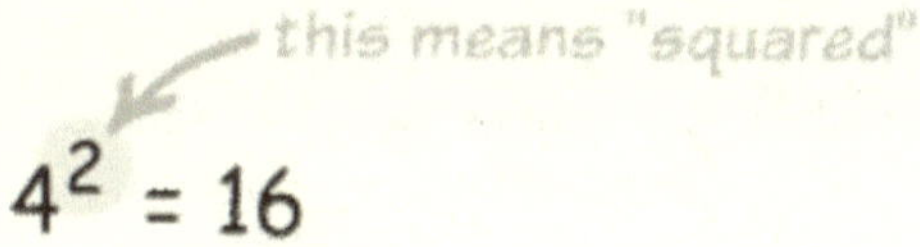

This says ***'4 Squared equals 16'*** (the little 2 says the number appears twice in multiplying)

Squares From 1^2 to 6^2

1 Squared	=	1^2	=	1×1	=	**1**
2 Squared	=	2^2	=	2×2	=	**4**
3 Squared	=	3^2	=	3×3	=	**9**
4 Squared	=	4^2	=	4×4	=	**16**
5 Squared	=	5^2	=	5×5	=	**25**
6 Squared	=	6^2	=	6×6	=	**36**

Negative Numbers

You can also square **negative numbers**.

Example: What happens when you square (-5)?

Answer:

$$(-5) \times (-5) = \mathbf{25}$$

(because a negative item gives a positive result)

When you square a **negative** number you get a **positive** result.

Just the same as if you had squared a positive number:

$$\left.\begin{aligned} 5\times5=25 \\ -5\times-5=25 \end{aligned}\right\}\text{same answers}$$

If someone says 'minus 5 squared' do you:

- Square the 5, then do the minus?
- Or do you square (-5)?

You get different answers:

Square 5, then do the minus:	Square (-5):
$-(5\times5) = -25$	$(-5)\times(-5) = +25$

Always make it clear what you mean, and that is what the '( )' are for.

Square Roots

A square root goes the other way:

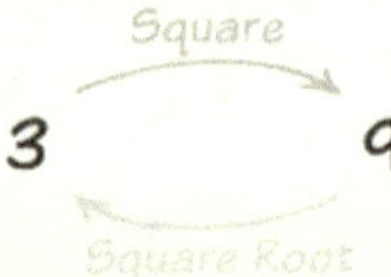

3 squared is 9, so a square root of 9 is 3

A square root of a number is ...

... a value that can be multiplied by itself to give the original number.

A square root of **9** is ...

... **3**, because when 3 is multiplied by itself you get 9.

It is like asking:

What can I multiply by itself to get this?

To help you remember think of the root of a tree:

'I know the tree, but what is the root that produced it?'

In this case the tree is '9', and the root is '3'.

Here are some more squares and square roots:

Square →		
← Square Root		
4		16
5		25
6		36

The Square Root Symbol

√ This is the special symbol that means 'square root', it is sort of like a tick, and actually started hundreds of years ago as a dot with a flick upwards.

It is called the *radical*, and always makes math look important!

You can use it like this:

$$\sqrt{9} = 3$$

you would say *'square root of 9 equals 3'*

Example: What is √25?

Well, we just happen to know that 25 = 5 × 5, so if you multiply 5 by itself (5 × 5) you will get 25.

So the answer is:

$$\sqrt{25} = 5$$

Example: What is √36 ?

Answer: 6 × 6 = 36, so √36 = 6

Perfect Squares

The perfect squares are the squares of the:

	1	2	3	4	5	6	7	8	9	10	11	12	13	14	15	etc
Perfect Squares:	**1**	**4**	**9**	**16**	**25**	**36**	**49**	**64**	**81**	**100**	**121**	**144**	**169**	**196**	**225**	**...**

Try to remember at least the first 10 of those.

A Fun Way to Calculate a Square Root

There is a fun method for calculating a square root that gets more and more accurate each time around:

(a) start with a guess (say 4 is the square root of 10)

(b) divide by the guess (10/4 = 2.5)

(c) add that to the guess (4 + 2.5 = 6.5)

(d) then divide *that* result by 2, in other words halve it. (6.5/2 = 3.25)

(e) now, set that as the new guess, and start at b) again

- Our first attempt got us from 4 to 3.25
- Going again (*b to e*) gets us: 3.163
- Going again (*b to e*) gets us: 3.1623

And so, after 3 times around the answer is 3.1623, which is pretty good, because:

$$3.1623 \times 3.1623 = 10.00014$$

How to Guess

What if you have to guess the square root for a difficult number such as '82,163' ... ?

In that case remember '82,163' has 5 digits, so the square root might have 3 digits (100x100=10,000), and the square root of 8 (the first digit) is about 3 (3x3=9), so 300 would be a good start.

Remember your formulae

Average formula:

Let $a_1, a_2, a_3, \ldots\ldots, a_n$ be a set of numbers, average

$$= (a_1 + a_2 + a_3, + \ldots\ldots + a_n)/n$$

Fractions formula:

Adding formula: $\frac{a}{b} + \frac{c}{d} = \frac{ad + bc}{bd}$

Subtracting formula: $\frac{a}{b} - \frac{c}{d} = \frac{ad - bc}{bd}$

Multiplying fractions: $\frac{a}{b} \times \frac{c}{d} = \frac{ac}{bd}$

Dividing fractions: $\frac{\frac{a}{b}}{\frac{c}{d}} = \frac{a}{b} \div \frac{c}{d} = \frac{a}{b} \times \frac{d}{c} = \frac{ad}{bc}$

Converting a mixed number to an improper fraction:

$$a\frac{c}{d}=\frac{ad+c}{d}$$

Converting an improper fraction to a mixed number:

$$\text{Divisor}\,\overline{)\,\text{Dividend}\,}\quad \text{Quotient Remainder}$$

Formula is: quotient $\dfrac{\text{Remainder}}{\text{Divisor}}$

Formula for a proportion:

$$\frac{a}{b}=\frac{c}{d}$$

In a proportion, the product of the extremes (ad) equal the product of the means (bc),

Thus, $ad = bc$

Percent:

Percent to fraction: x% = x/100

Percentage formula: Rate/100 = Percentage/base

Rate: The percent

Base: The amount you are taking the percent of

Percentage: The answer obtained by multiplying the base by the rate

Consumer math formula:

Discount =list price × discount rate

Sale price =list price – discount

Discount rate = discount ÷ list price

Sales tax =price of item × tax rate

Interest =principal × rate of interest × time

Tips =cost of meals × tip rate

Commission =cost of service × commission rate

Geometry formula:

Perimeter:

Perimeter of a square: s + s + s + s

s: length of one side

Perimeter of a rectangle: l + w + l + w

l: length

w: width

Perimeter of a triangle: a + b + c

a, b, and c: lengths of the 3 sides

Area:

Area of a square: s × s

s: length of one side

Area of a rectangle: l × w

l: length

w: width

Area of a triangle: (b × h)/2

b: length of base

h: length of height

Area of a trapezoid: $(b_1 + b_2) \times h/2$

b_1 and b_2: parallel sides or the bases

h: length of height

Volume:

Volume of a cube: s × s × s

s: length of one side

Volume of a box: l × w × h

l: length

w: width

h: height

Volume of a sphere: (4/3) × pi × r^3

pi: 3.14

r: radius of sphere

Volume of a triangular prism: area of triangle × Height = (1/2 base × height) × Height

base: length of the base of the triangle

height: height of the triangle

Height: height of the triangular prism

Volume of a cylinder: pi × r^2 × Height

pi: 3.14

r: radius of the circle of the base

Height: height of the cylinder

Algebra formulae:

1. **$(a + b)(a - b) = a^2 - b^2$**
2. **$(a + b + c)^2 = a^2 + b^2 + c^2 + 2(ab + bc + ca)$**
3. **$(a \pm b)^2 = a^2 + b^2 \pm 2ab$**
4. **$(a + b + c + d)^2 = a^2 + b^2 + c^2 + d^2 + 2(ab + ac + ad + bc + bd + cd)$**
5. **$(a \pm b)^3 = a^3 \pm b^3 \pm 3ab(a \pm b)$**
6. **$(a \pm b)(a^2 + b^2$ m $ab) = a^3 \pm b^3$**
7. **$(a + b + c)(a^2 + b^2 + c^2 - ab - bc - ca) = a^3 + b^3 + c^3 - 3abc$**

Know the shapes

Equilateral Triangle

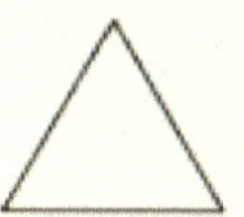

Equilateral triangles have all angles equal to 60°, and all sides of equal length.

All equilateral triangles have 3 lines of symmetry.

Isoscles Triangle

Isosceles triangles have 2 angles equal and 2 sides of equal length.

All isosceles triangles have a line of symmetry.

Scalene Triangle

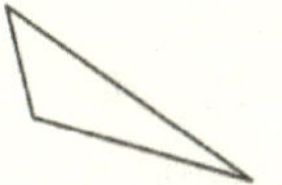

Scalene triangles have no angles equal, and no sides of equal length.

Right Triangle

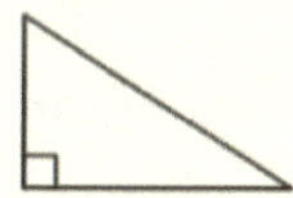

Right triangles (or right angled triangles) have one right angle (equal to 90°).

Obtuse Triangle

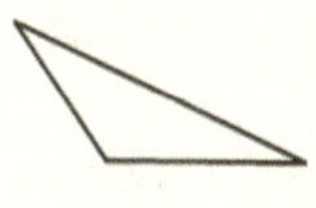

Obtuse triangles have one obtuse angle (an angle greater than 90°). The other two angles are acute (less than 90°).

Acute Triangle

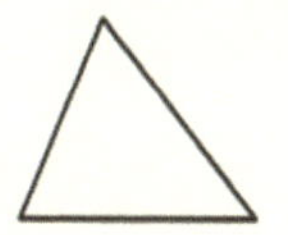

Acute triangles have all angles acute.

Square

Squares have 4 equal sides and 4 right angles.

They have 4 lines of symmetry.

All squares belong to the rectangle family.

All squares belong to the rhombus family.

All squares are also parallelograms.

Rectangle

Rectangles have 4 sides and 4 right angles.

They all have 2 lines of symmetry (4 lines if they are also a square!)

All rectangles belong to the parallelogram family.

Rhombus

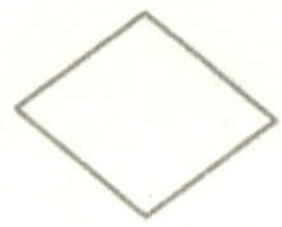

Rhombuses (rhombii) have 4 equal sides.

Both pairs of opposite sides are parallel.

They all have 2 lines of symmetry (4 lines if they are a square!)

All rhombuses belong to the parallelogram family.

Parallelogram

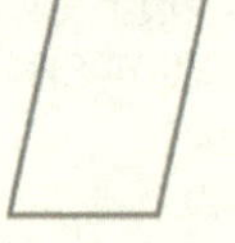

Parallelograms have 2 pairs of parallel sides.

Some parallelograms have lines of symmetry (depending on whether they are also squares, rectangles or rhombuses), but most do not.

Trapezoid US (Trapezium UK)

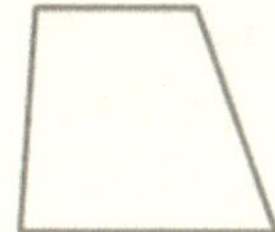

Trapezoids US (Trapeziums UK) have one pair of parallel sides.
Some trapezoids have a line of symmetry.

Kite

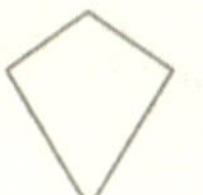

Kites have 2 pairs of equal sides, which are adjacent to each other.

Trapezium US (Trapezoid UK)

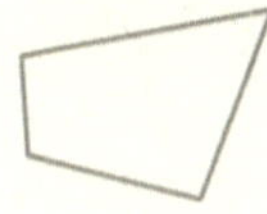

Trapeziums US (Trapezoids UK) are quadrilaterals with no parallel sides

Please note the differences between the definitions for US and UK.

Regular and Irregular Polygons

2. Here is a list of regular polygons from 3 to 10 sides.
3. For each polygon, a regular and an irregular example have been shown.
4. Any regular shape will be mathematically similar to the example shown (having the same angles).
5. There are an infinite number of examples of different irregular polygons that could be shown, and only one example is given.

Equilateral Triangle

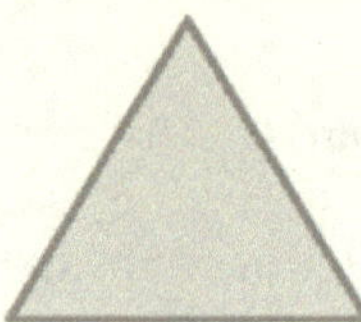

Angle: 60°

Interior angles add up to 180°

Irregular Triangle

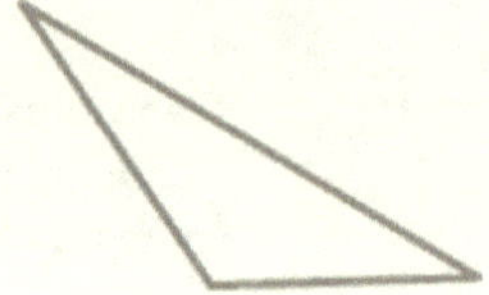

Square

Angle: 90°

Interior angles add up to 360°

Irregular Quadrilateral

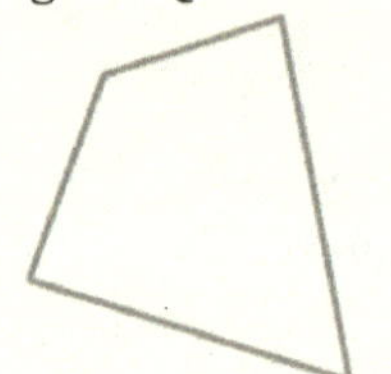

Pentagon

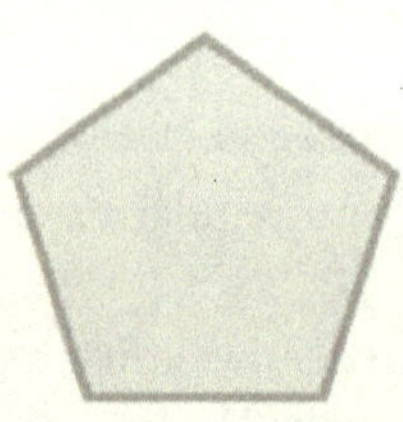

Angle: 108°

Interior angles add up to 540°

Irregular Pentagon

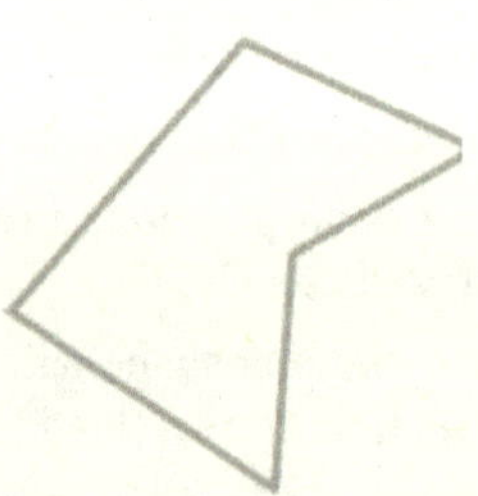

Hexagon

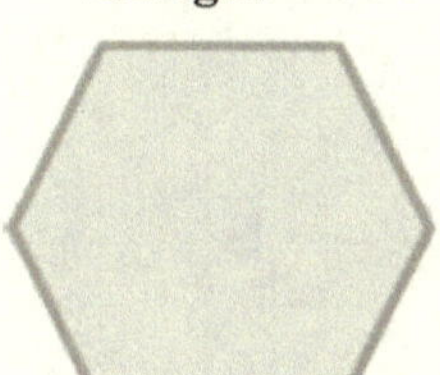

Irregular Hexagon

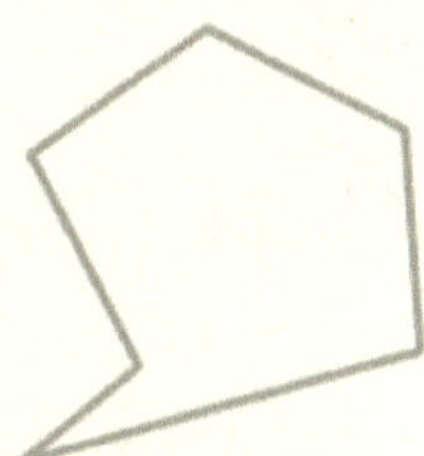

Angle: 120°
Interior angles add up to 720°

Heptagon

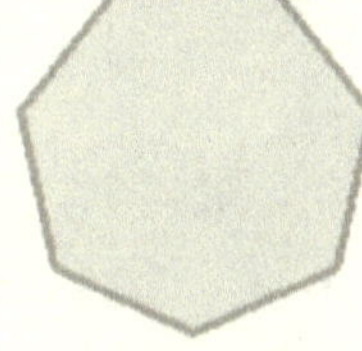

Irregular Heptagon

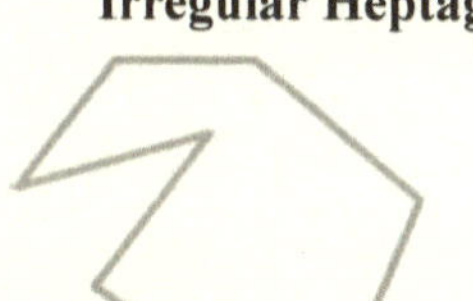

Angle: 128.6°
Interior angles add up to 900°

Octagon

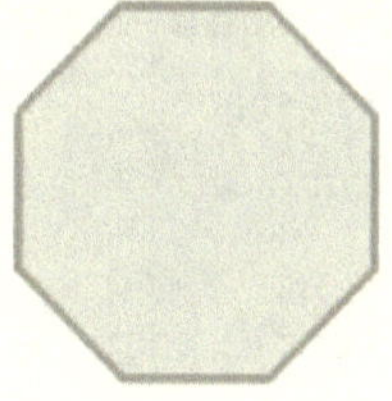

Irregular Octagon

Angle: 135°
Interior angles add up to 1080°

Nonagon

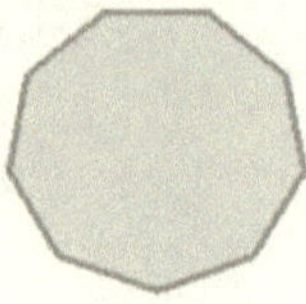

Angle: 140°

Interior angles add up to 1260°

Irregular Nonagon

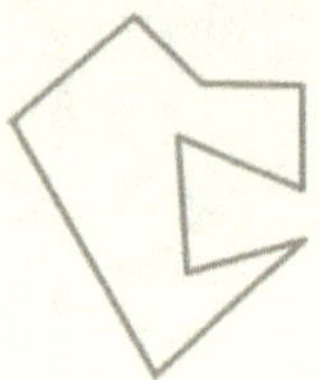

Decagon

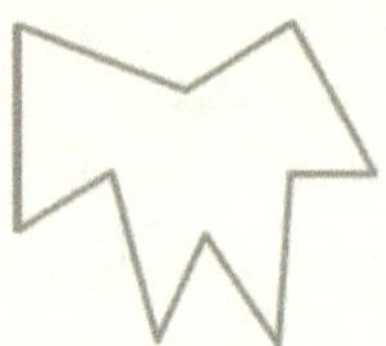

Angle: 144°

Interior angles add up to 1440°

Irregular Decagon

Cube

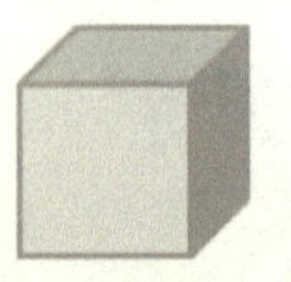

Cubes have 6 faces, 12 edges and 8 vertices.

All sides on a cube are equal length.

All faces are square in shape.

A cube is a type of cuboid.

Cuboid

Cuboids have 6 faces, 12 edges and 8 vertices.

All the faces on a cuboid are rectangular.

Sphere

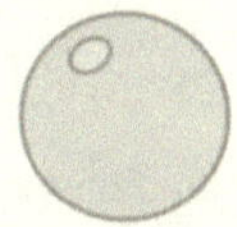

Spheres have 1 curved face, 0 edges and 0 vertices.

Cylinder

Closed Cylinders have 3 faces, 2 edges and 0 vertices.

Closed cylinders have 2 circular or elliptical faces and one curved rectangular face.

Cones

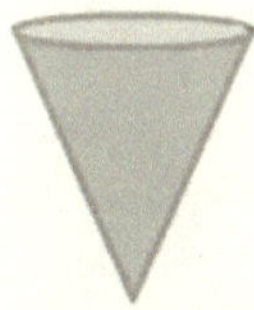

Cones have 2 faces, 1 edge and 1 apex (which is described by some mathematicians as a vertex).

Triangular Prism

Triangular Prisms have 5 faces, 9 edges, and 6 vertices. The two faces at either end are triangles, and the rest of the faces are rectangular.

Hexagonal Prism

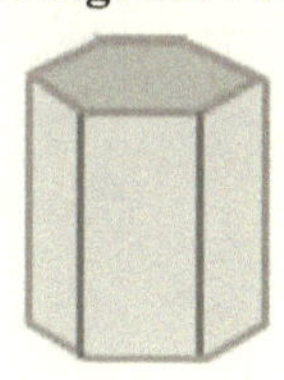

Hexagonal Prisms have 8 faces, 18 edges, and 12 vertices.

The two faces at either end are hexagons, and the rest of the faces are rectangular.

Triangular-based Pyramid

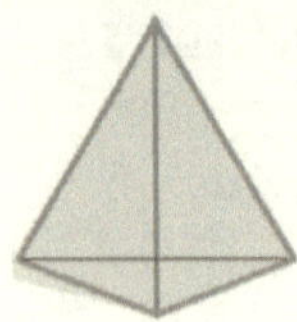

Triangular-based pyramids have 4 faces, 6 edges and 4 vertices.

The base is a triangle. All of the faces are triangular.

Square-based Pyramid

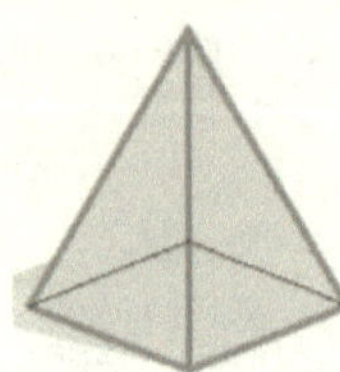

Square based pyramids have 5 faces, 8 edges and 5 vertices

The base is a square. All the other faces are triangular.

Hexagonal Pyramid

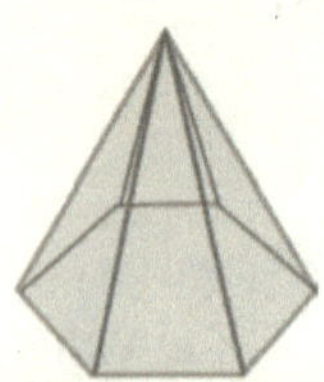

Hexagonal pyramids have 7 faces, 12 edges and 7 vertices.

The base is a hexagon. All of the other faces are triangular.

Be smart with the Rubic's cube!

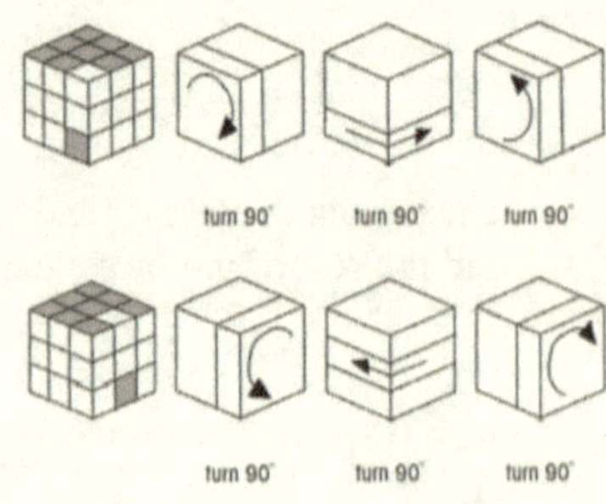

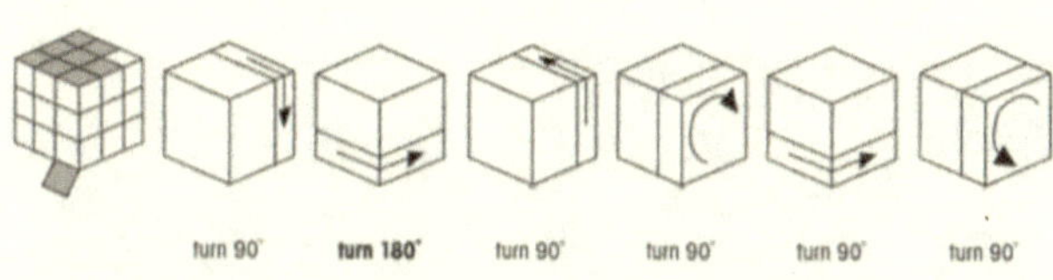

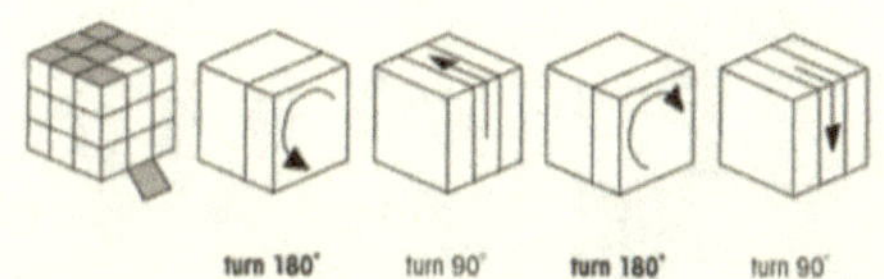

Now you have the top of the cube as all one colour!

The next step is to get all the surrounding edge colours the same and for them to match their corresponding centre colours. This creates a T shape as indicated below.

There are two solutions to achieve the above stage. Follow the one that applies.

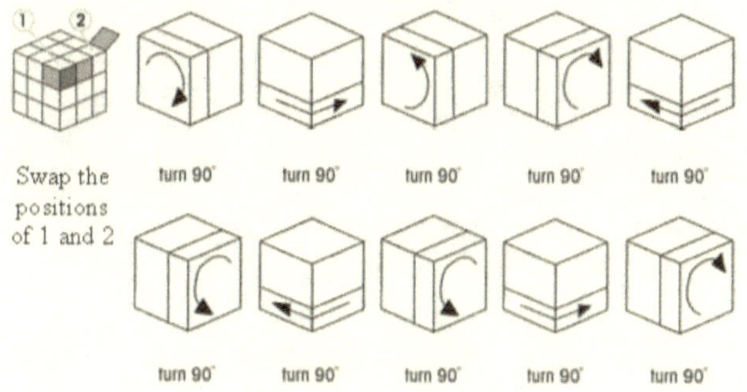

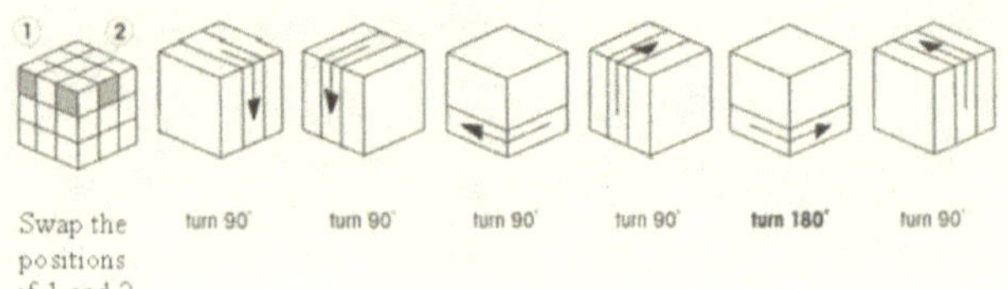

The next stage is to complete 2 layers of the cube. As above. To achieve this stage you must now turn your cube upside down. The T shape now turned on its head. Again there are two methods of achieving this next stage. You may need to use one or both methods to complete.

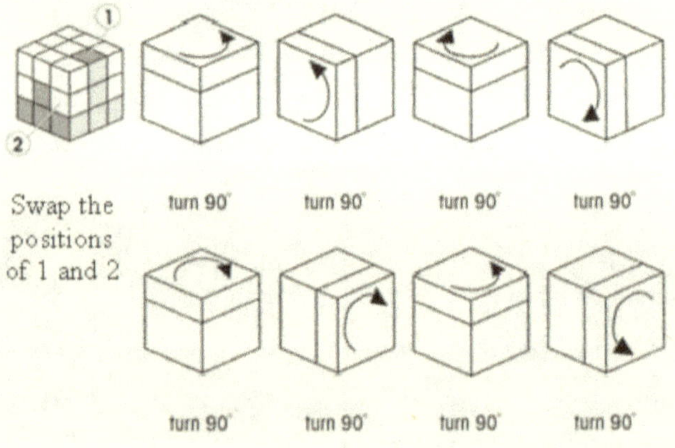

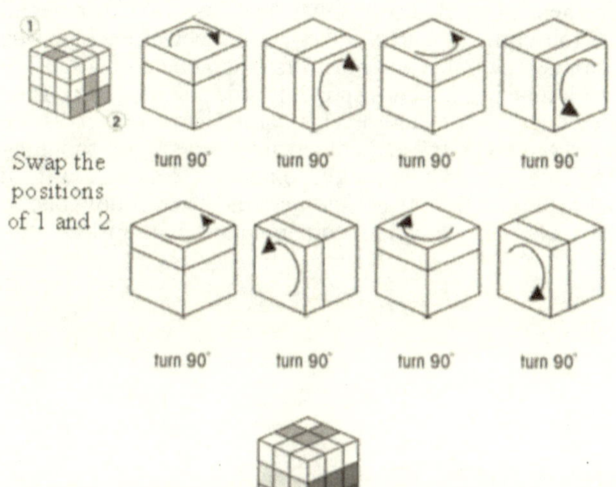

Now, follow the next set of moves to achieve a cross shape on the top of the cube as indicated below. Keep turning the cube as indicated below until an L shape appears as above. Keeping this L shape in the position above (furthest away from you). In this position, you will only need to follow the next set of moves, once again, to achieve the cross.

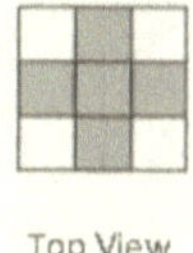

Top View

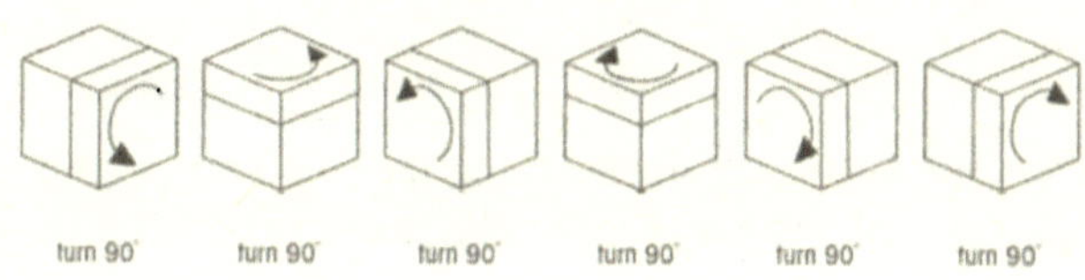

The next stage of how to solve the rubiks cube is to get all the top corner squares, matching the corresponding side colours. To do this you must first align one corner only so that it matches it's corresponding side colours (this corner may not match exactly). This corner is then taken as the reference point. If 2 or 3 corners match their corresponding side colours then keep making either of the moves outlined below until only one corner matches. Then follow one of the steps below to get all corners in the right position.

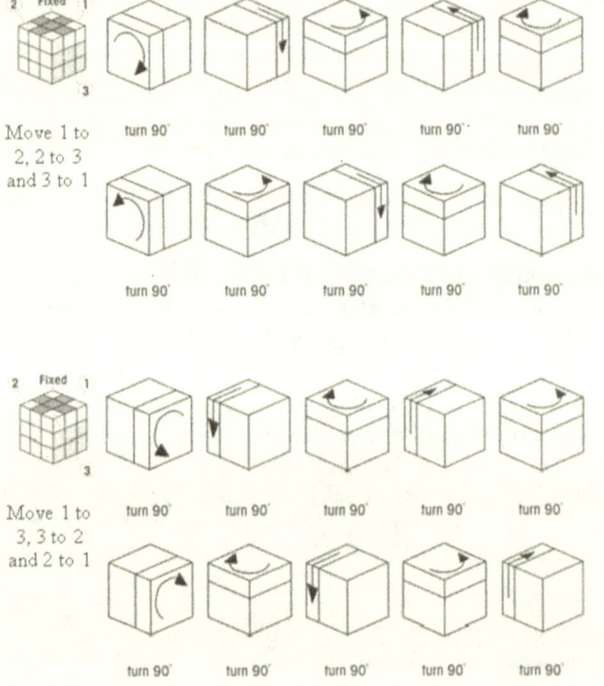

When all four top corners are in their correct positions (although colours may not align) proceed to either or both of the next stages. Now your reference point has changed again. Keep the corner that is correct in it's position as indicated 'fixed' as you turn the planes according to the following moves.

This set of moves rotates three of the four corners.

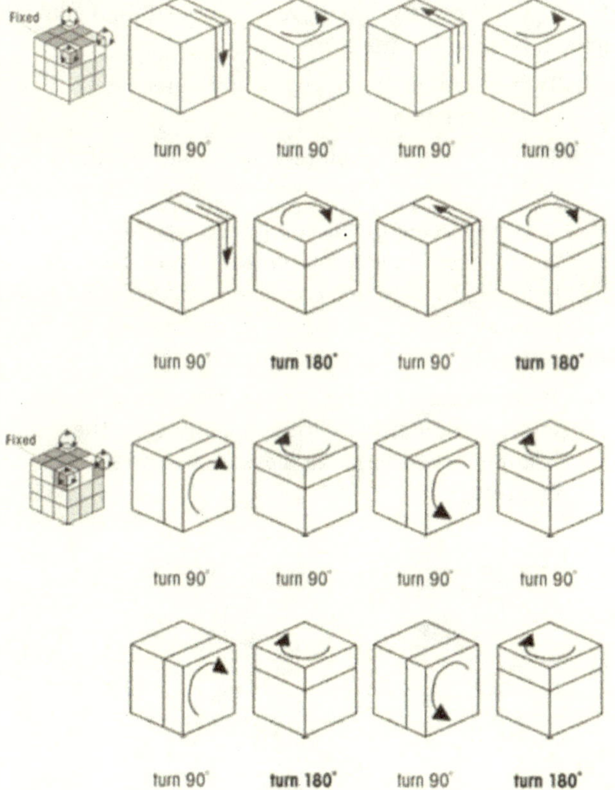

You may find that you have already completed the cube at this stage. If however, you have not you will find yourself in the following position:

1. Two or Three of the top centre squares are in the correct position
2. Three of the top centre squares are in the wrong position.

1. If two or three of the top centre squares are in the correct position, you must make the moves as indicated below until only one centre square is in the correct position then follow the moves once or twice more to complete the cube.
2. With one centre colour in its correct position make the moves indicated below to complete the cube. You may need to make these moves a few times to complete.

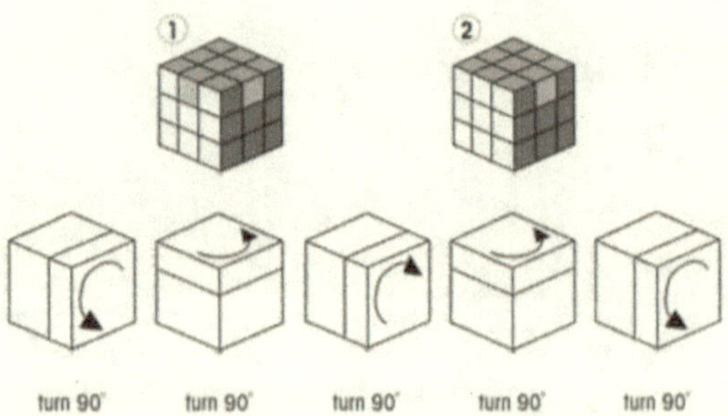

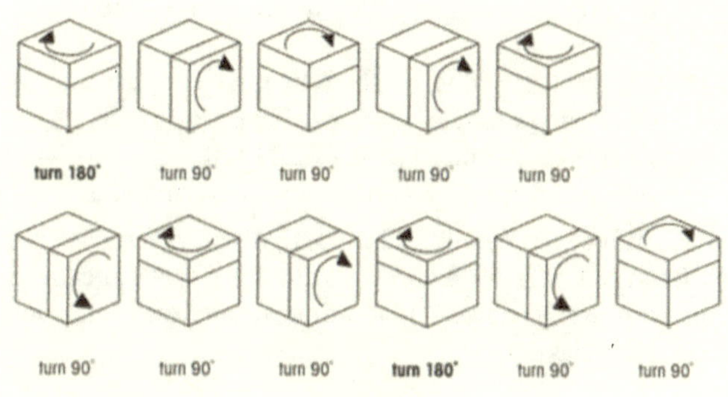

3 Unsual Mental Math Tricks

1. The Trick of The 11s.

When multiplying a two digit number by 11, the result is always first digit of the number, sum of the two numbers, aad the last digit. Example: 11 x 18 is 198. 11 x 32 is 352. If the sum of the digits comes out greater than nine, add one to the first digit. 11 × 78 is 858.

2. At what age should you get married?

This one uses the Euler's number (e, which roughly equals 2.71828) to tell you the age where you have the highest probability of getting married to the ideal person.

* Figure out the age range when you consider yourself

eligible for marriage. If you're already well into it, let's say 22 to 45.

* Subtract the oldest age from the youngest age to calculate your total number of marryin' years.
* Divide that number by e, or 2.71828.
* Add the result to your youngest marrying age.

So if you've set a range of 22 to 45, that's 23 years. Divided by Eular's number is 8.46. Added to 22 is 30.46, meaning that between 30 and 31 is the time when you're at your statistical peak.

3. The 111 tricks

* Take the last two digits of the year you were born.
* Add that to the age you're going to turn (or you've already turned) here in 2011.
* The result should be... 111.

Numbers and Division

Dividing by 1

You wanna divide a number by one, do you? Easy. Take the number - say 3,3892 - and that's it. That's your answer. 429 / 1 = 429. 11 / 1 = 11. 1,000,000 ? 1 / 1,000,000.

Dividing by 2

When you divide something by two, you simply cut it in half. Half of 234 is 117, therefore 234 / 2 = 117. Let's try a smaller number: 20 / 2 = 10. Why? Because half of 20 is 10. If the number you're trying to divide is odd (like, say, 33), then you can't divide it evenly by two.

Dividing by 3

Wanna know if you can divide a number evenly by three? Just add up all the digits until you have a single number. If that number is divisible by three, so is the original number. Case in point: 8787. If you add 8+7+8+7 you get 30. Then add 3+0, which equals three. Three is definitely divisible by three, so you know that 8787 is too.

Dividing by 4

The rule for dividing by four is the same as for dividing by two - only you have to do it twice. If you want to divide 88 by 4, you simply halve 88 (which is 44) and then halve that number (which, in this case, is 22). Half of 12 is six and half of six is three - so your answer is three.

Dividing by 5

If you want to know whether a number can be evenly divided by five you just need to look at the number's last digit. If the last digit is a zero or a five, then the number is divisible by five. 1,573,740 ends in zero so it is divisible by five. Since 23 ends in three, it isn't divisible by five.

Dividing by 6

If a number is both divisible by three (see the three rule) AND an even number (ending in 0, 2, 4, 6 or 8) then it is divisible by six too. 312 is an even number and if you add up all the digits they equal six, which is divisible by three. Therefore, 312 is divisible by six.

Dividing by 7

To find out if a number is divisible by seven, take the last digit, double it, and subtract it from the rest of the number.

If you had 203, you would double the last digit (three) to get six, and subtract that from 20 (the remaining amount) to get 14. Since 14 is divisible by seven, 203 is too.

Dividing by 8

This brings us back to the old halving trick we used with two and four. Try halving four times to get the answer to this one. Want an example? Okay. 64 ? 8. Half of 64 is 32 and half of 32 is 16, then half of 16 is 8. Therefore, 64 ? 8 = 8.

Dividing by 9

Use the same trick we used to see if a number is divisible by three - it works for any power of three (3, 6, 9, 12, etc.).

Dividing by 10

If a number is evenly divisible by 10 it will end in zero. Simply remove that zero to find out what that number would be if it were divided by 10. Example: 370 / 10 = 37 (which is 370 with the '0' taken off the end). 50 / 10 = 5. See

Multiplication Table Tricks

Zero and One Times Tables

Check this out: if you multiply ANYTHING by zero, the answer is zero. Anything. 4 x 0 = 0 and 1,000,000 x 0 = 0. One times tables are almost as easy. Any number multiplied by one is always itself. 'Huh,' you say? Well, check it out: 1 x 10 = 10, 1 x 42 = 42, 8,726 x 1 = 8,726.

Two Times Tables

When you multiply a number by two, you just double that

number. That's some pretty simple math, even for the most numerically challenged of us. So, if you want to figure out what 2 x 7 is, you just add 7 + 7 (the answer is 14, by the way). Any number times two is the same as that number PLUS itself. Here's one more example: 2 x 5 is the same as 5 + 5, which equals 10.

Four Times Tables: When you multiply four with anything, you have to use the doubling-up trick (that's the one you used for the two times table) twice. Here's an example: 4 x 7 is the same as 7 + 7 = 14 and then 14 + 14 = 28. So 4 x 7 = 28. Here's another double example: 4 x 10 is the same as 10 + 10 = 20, so then 20 + 20 = 40. So the answer is 4 x 10 = 40.

Five Times Tables

When you want to multiply a number by five you just count up by fives that may times. Let's review how to count by fives: 5, 10, 15, 20, 25...and so on. Got it? So if you want to multiply 5 x 7, you just count by fives, seven times. 5, 10, 15, 20, 25, 30, 35. So 7 x 5 = 35. If you have trouble keeping track, just use your fingers.

Nine Times Tables

For this method you are going to need to have two hands. Put your hands in front of you with your palms towards you. Your fingers represent the numbers one to ten (one is your left thumb; ten is your right thumb). Now you're ready to do your nine times tables. Let's say the question is 9 x 4. Count to the fourth finger (if you've counted right, it will be the ring finger on your left hand) and curl that finger under. Now you have three fingers up before that finger and 6 up after it. So the answer is 36. Let's try 9 x 8. Put down the 8th finger (middle finger on the right hand) so that you have seven fingers up before the finger you curled under, and two fingers afterward. So the answer is 72.

Ten Times Tables

If you want to multiply something by 10, just add a zero at the end. Here's an example: 10 x 8 = 80 or 10 x 100 = 1,000. Try it with any number - from one to a billion.

Eleven Times Tables

Any number - up to nine - multiplied by 11 is itself written out twice. Confused? Just check it out: 9 x 11 = 99, 4 x 11 = 44, 3 x 11 = 33 and so on.

Make it quick!

Multiply Up to 20X20 In Your Head

With this trick, you will be able to multiply any two numbers from 11 to 19 in your head quickly, without the use of a calculator.

Try this:

Take 15 x 13 for an example.

Always place the larger number of the two on top in your mind.

Then draw the shape of Africa mentally so it covers the 15 and the 3 from the 13 below. Those covered numbers are all you need.

First add 15 + 3 = 18

Add a zero behind it (multiply by 10) to get 180.

Multiply the covered lower 3 x the single digit above it the '5' (3 x 5 = 15)

Add 180 + 15 = 195

The 11 Rule

You should be able to do this one in you head for any two digit number. Practice it on paper first! To multiply any two digit number by 11:

For this example we will use 54.

Separate the two digits in you mind (5__4).

Notice the hole between them!

Add the 5 and the 4 together (5 + 4 = 9)

Put the resulting 9 in the hole 594. That's it! 11 x 54=594

The only thing tricky to remember is that if the result of the addition is greater than 9, you only put the 'ones' digit in the hole and carry the 'tens' digit from the addition. For example 11 x 57 ... 5__7 ... 5+7=12 ... put the 2 in the hole and add the 1 from the 12 to the 5 in to get 6 for a result of 627 ... 11 x 57 = 627

Square a 2 Digit ending in 5

For this example we will use 25

Take the 'tens' part of the number (the 2 and add 1)=3

Multiply the original 'tens' part of the number by the new number (2x3)

Take the result (2x3=6) and put 25 behind it. Result is the answer 625

Try a few more 75 squared ... = 7x8=56 ... put 25 behind it is 5625

55 squared = 5x6=30 ... put 25 behind it ... is 3025. Another easy one! Practice it on paper first!

Square 2 digit-numbers

Square a 2 Digit Number, for this example take 37:

Look for the nearest 10 boundary

In this case up 3 from 37 to 40.

Since you went UP 3 to 40 go DOWN 3 from 37 to 34.

Now mentally multiply 34x40

The way I do it is 34x10=340

Double it mentally to 680

Double it again mentally to 1360

This 1360 is the FIRST interim answer

37 is '3' away from the 10 boundary 40

Square this '3' distance from 10 boundary

3x3=9 which is the SECOND interim answer

Add the two interim answers to get the final answer

Answer: 1360 + 9 = 1369

Multiply by 4

To quickly multiply by four, double the number and then double it again.

Often this can be done in your head.

Multiply by 5

To quickly multiply by 5, divide the number in two and then multiply it by 10. Often this can be done quickly in your head.

The 11 Rule expanded

You can directly write down the answer to any number multiplied by 11

Take for example the number 51236 × 11

First, write down the number with a zero in front of it.

051236

The zero is necessary so that the rules are simpler.

Draw a line under the number.

Bear with me on this one. It is simple if you work through it slowly. To do this, all you have to do is 'Add the neighbor'. Look at the 6 in the 'units' position of the number. Since there is no number to the right of it, you can't add to its 'neighbor' so just write down 6 below the 6 in the units col.

For the 'tens' place, add the 3 to the its 'neighbor' (the 6). Write the answer: 9 below 3.

For the 'hundreds' place, add the 2 to the its 'neighbor' (the 3). Write the answer: 5 below 2.

For the 'thousands' place, add the 1 to the its 'neighbor' (the 2). Write the answer: 3 below 1.

For the 'ten-thousands' place, add the 5 to the its 'neighbor' (the 1). Write the answer: 6 below 5.

For the 'hundred-thousands' place, add the 0 to the its 'neighbor' (the 5). Write the answer: 5 below 0.

That's it ... 11 X 051236 = 563596

To calculate reminder on dividing the number by 27 and 37

Understand this rule by taking examples

Consider number 34568276, we have to calculate the reminder on dividing this number by 27 and 37 respectively.

Make triplets as written below starting from the units place

34.........568..........276

now sum of all triplets = 34+568+276 = 878

divide it by 27, we get reminder as 14

divide it by 37, we get reminder as 27

Example:

Other examples for the clarification of the rule

let the number be 2387850765

triplets are 2...387...850...765

sum of the triplets = 2+387+850+765 = 2004

on revising the steps we get

2......004

sum = 6

divide it by 27, we get reminder as 6

divide it by 37, we get reminder as 6

To calculate reminder on dividing the number by 7, 11, 13

Consider number 34568276, we have to calculate the reminder on dividing this number by 7, 11, 13 respectively.

make triplets as written below starting from the units place

34.........568..........276

now alternate sum = 34+276 = 310 and 568

and difference of these sums = 568-310 = 258

divide it by 7 we get reminder as 6

divide it by 11 we get reminder as 5

divide it by 13 we get reminder as 11

Method: first calculate the digit sum, then divide it by 3, the reminder in this case will be the required reminder

Example:

1342568

let the number be as written above

its digit sum = 29 = 11 = 2

so reminder will be 2

Example:

Take some others

34259677858

digit sum of the number is 64 = 10 = 1

reminder is 1

similarly let the number be 54670329845

then digit sum = 53 = 8

when we divide 8 by 3 we get reminder as 2 so answer will be 2

To calculate reminder on dividing the number by 3

Method: first calculate the digit sum, then divide it by 3, the reminder in this case will be the required reminder

Example:

1342568

let the number be as written above

its digit sum = 29 = 11 = 2

so reminder will be 2

Example:

Take some others

34259677858

digit sum of the number is 64 = 10 = 1

reminder is 1

similarly let the number be 54670329845

then digit sum = 53 = 8

when we divide 8 by 3 we get reminder as 2 so answer will be 2.

Some Basic Addition TIPS

Adding 0

If you understand that when you add zero you add nothing, you should never get a basic fact with zero wrong. Make sure this understanding is in place.

Adding 1

Adding one means saying the larger number, then jumping up one number, or counting up one number. This happens every time you add one. It never changes. Never recount the larger number, just say it and count up one.

Example:

6 + 1 = say 6 then 7

44 + 1 = say 44 then 45

Adding 2

Adding two means saying the larger number, then jumping up or counting up twice. Again, this is always correct and never changes.

Example:

9 + 2 = say 9 then 10 then 11

45 + 2 say 45 then 46 then 47

Adding 10

Adding ten means jumping up ten (think of a hundred's chart). The ones digit stays the same, but the ten's digit increases by one. We must understand this. Using a hundreds board to teach this works well to build understanding. We actually count up the ten and write down the result. Then affirm with them the pattern and explain why it works every time.

Example:

5 + 10 = 15

10 + 7 = 17

Example:

23 + 10 = 33

48 + 10 = 58

Adding 9

Adding 9 makes sense if one understands how to add ten. It sounds more difficult than it actually is.

Remember the jump of ten – 5 + 10 = 15. A student would say (in their head) '5 plus 10 = fifteen'.

The five and fifteen are naming the same number of ones.

With the nines – a student must count down one in the ones.

A student would say '5 + 9 = fourteen'.

It sounds difficult, but once they catch on it is really simple.

Work with lots of examples until the idea is understood:

5 + 10 = fifteen 5 + 9 = fourteen 7 + 10 = 17 7 + 9 = sixteen

Adding 8

This works exactly the same, only a child must think 2 less. Using the examples above students would say; 5 + 10 = 15 so 5 +8 = 13, 7 + 10 = 17 so 7 + 8 = 15 (2 less)

Double Numbers

To add double numbers there are a couple of strategies that might help students.

When you add a double you are counting by that number once.

For example:

4 + 4 = think of 4, 8 … counting by fours

Practice skip counting by each number in turn:

2-4

3-6

4-8 etc. This gets harder with the higher numbers, but skip counting is an important skill for students to have.

Doubles occur everywhere in life.

For example:

An egg carton is 6 + 6

two hands are 5 + 5

16 pack of crayons has 8 + 8

two weeks 7 + 7

Do a variety of activities with double numbers and have students determine and explain, which strategies help them remember. Each one should look at each fact and relate to a visual image or counting by strategy that works for them.

Near Doubles

To use the near doubles strategy a student first has to master the doubles. Then, if the double is known, they use that and count up or down one to find the near double.

Example:

4 + 4 = 8 so 5 + 4 = 9 (count up one)

Or: 4 + 4 = 8 so 4 + 3 = 7 (count down one)

Adding 5

Adding five has a strategy that is helpful, but not completely effective as it is a bit tricky. You can decide if it is helpful or not.

To add fives look for the five in both numbers to make a ten then count on the extra digits.

Example:

5 + 7 = (10 + 2) = 12

5 + 8 = 5 + 5 + 3 = 13

Students who can see the five in 8 should have no difficulty. Students who can't visualize numbers will find this hard. Most students can be taught to do this with some extra work.

Subtraction

Left -To- Right Subtraction

Subtraction can become almost as easy as addition: compute from left to right and break down problems into simpler components.

Two-digit Subtraction

While subtracting two-digit numbers we must try to simplify the problem so that it is reduced to subtracting (or adding) a one-digit number.

Here's a simple subtraction problem:

$$\begin{array}{rl} & 76 \\ - & 25\,(20+5) \\ \hline \end{array}$$

First subtract 20 (76-20 = 56) then we subtract 5 to reach the simpler subtraction problem 56-5 for your answer of 51. The problem can be seen this way.

$$76-25 \;=\; 56-5=51$$

(First subtract 20)   (Then subtract 5).

$$\begin{array}{rl} & 76 \\ - & 25\,(20+5) \\ \hline \end{array}$$

First subtract 20 (76-20 = 56) then we subtract 5 to reach the simpler subtraction problem 56-5 for your answer of 51. The problem can be seen this way.

$$76 - 25 = 56 - 5 = 51$$

(First subtract 20) (Then subtract 5)

Remember: 'Hard' subtraction problems can usually be turned into 'easy' addition problems.

Here's another:

$$\begin{array}{r} 86 \\ -\ 29\ (20+9) \text{ or } (30-1) \\ \hline \end{array}$$

There are two different ways to solve this problem mentally:

First subtract 20, then subtract 9:

$$86 - 29 = 66 - 9 = 57$$

(First subtract 20) (Then subtract 9)

Follow this strategy:

First subtract 30, then add back 1:

$$86 - 29 = 56 + 1 = 57$$

(First subtract 30) (then add 1)

Subtraction of two digits with carry forward:

$$\begin{array}{r} 86 \\ -\ 29\ (20+9) \text{ or } (30-1) \\ \hline \end{array}$$

First subtract 20 from 86. Then subtract 9 from the total. This way:

$$86 - 29 = 66 - 9 = 57$$

Subtraction of three digits without carry forward

$$
\begin{array}{l}
958 \\
-\ 417\ (400 + 10 + 7)
\end{array}
$$

Now, this is how you need to do this:

$$958 - 400 = 558 - 10 = 548 - 7 = 541$$

Subtraction of three digits with carry forward

$$
\begin{array}{l}
747 \\
-\ 598\ (600 - 2)
\end{array}
$$

Now, this is how you need to do this:

$$747 - 600 = 147 + 2 = 149$$

Check one more out:

$$
\begin{array}{l}
853 \\
-\ 692\ (700–2)
\end{array}
$$

Now, this is how you need to do this:

$$853 - 700 = 153 + 8 = 161$$

Instant Multiplication

Multiply, in your head, any two-digit number by eleven. Here is the SECRET: It's easy once you know the secret. Consider the problem:

$$42 \times 11$$

To solve this problem, simply add the digits, 4 + 2 = 6, put the 6 between the 3 and the 2, and there is your answer: 362.

Try the next

53×11

To solve this problem, simply add the digits, 5 + 3 = 9, put the 9 between the 3 and the 2, and there is your answer:

392

Since 5+ 3 = 8, your answer is simply

81 × 11?

WITHOUT A PEN OR PAPER or finger count,

81 x 11?

Did you get 891? Congratulations!

Suppose the problem is

85 x 11

Beware: Although 8+5=13,The answer is NOT 8135!

As before, the 3 goes in between the numbers, but the 1needs to be added to the 8 to get the correct answer:

935

Think of the problem this way:

$$\begin{array}{r} 1 \\ +\ 835 \\ \hline =\ 935 \\ \hline \end{array}$$

Here is another example. Try 57 x 11.

Since 5 + 7 = 12, the answer is

$$\begin{array}{r} 1 \\ +\ 527 \\ \hline =\ 627 \\ \hline \end{array}$$

Now do it as fast as you can.......................

77 x 11?

Did you get 847? CONGRATS!

So now we are equipped in our head, any two-digit number by eleven. But watch out: 99 x 11. Let's do this NOW:

Since 9 + 9 = 18, the answer is:

$$\begin{array}{r} 1 \\ +\ 989 \\ \hline =\ 1089 \\ \hline \end{array}$$

Now comes the crucial question: what if we are multiplying three-digit numbers (or larger) by eleven... Can we use this method?

YES

314 × 11

The answer still begins with 3 and ends with 4. Since 3 + 1 = 4, and 1+ 4= 5, the answer is 3454.

Division made easy

Step 1: Division is even in all the digits

We divide numbers where each of the hundreds, tens,

and ones digits are evenly divisible by the divisor. The GOAL in this first, easy step is to get students used to two things:

1. To get used to the long division 'corner' so that the quotient is written on top.
2. To get used to asking how many times does the divisor go into the various digits of the dividend.

Example problems for this step follow. Students should check each division by multiplication.

(a) $4\overline{)8\,4}$

(b) $3\overline{)6\,6\,0}$

(c) $4\overline{)8\,0\,4\,0}$

Students also learn in this step to look at the first two digits of the dividend, if the divisor does not 'go into' the first digit:

$$\begin{array}{r} \text{h t o} \\ 0 \\ 4\overline{)2\,4\,8} \end{array}$$

$$\begin{array}{r} \text{h t o} \\ 0\,6\,2 \\ 4\overline{)2\,4\,8} \end{array}$$

4 does not go into 2. You can put zero in the quotient in the hundreds place or omit it. But 4 does go into 24, six times. Put 6 in the quotient.

Explanation:

The 2 of 248 is of course 200 in reality. If you divided 200 by 4, the result would be less than 100, so that is why the quotient won't have any whole hundreds.

But then you combine the 2 hundreds with the 4 tens. That makes 24 tens, and you CAN divide 24 tens by 4. The result 6 tens goes as part of the quotient.

Check the final answer: $4 \times 62 = 248$.

More example problems follow. Divide. Check your answer by multiplying the quotient and the divisor.

(a) $3\overline{)1\,2\,3}$

(b) $4\overline{)2\,8\,4}$

(c) $6\overline{)3\,6\,0}$

(d) $8\overline{)2\,4\,8}$

Step 2: A Remainder in the ones

Now, there is a remainder in the ones (units). Thousands, hundreds, and tens digits still divide evenly by the divisor. First, students can solve the remainder *mentally* and simply write the remainder right after the quotient:

```
    h t o
    0 4 1 R1
 4 ) 1 6 5
```

4 does not go into 1 (hundred). So combine the 1 hundred with the 6 tens (160).

4 goes into 16 four times.

4 goes into 5 once, leaving a remainder of 1.

```
    t h t o
    0 4 0 0 R7
 8 ) 3 2 0 7
```

8 does not go into 3 of the thousands. So combine the 3 thousands with the 2 hundreds (3,200).

8 goes into 32 four times (3,200 ÷ 8 = 400)
8 goes into 0 zero times (tens).
8 goes into 7 zero times, and leaves a remainder of 7.

Next, students learn to **find the remainder using the process of 'multiply & subtract'**. This is a very important step! The 'multiply & subtract' part is often very confusing to students, so here we practice it in the easiest possible place: in the very end of the division, in the ones colum (instead of in the tens or hundreds column). Of course, this assumes that students have already learned to find the remainder in easy division problems that are based on the multiplication tables (such as 45 ÷ 7 or 18 ÷ 5).

In the problems before, you just wrote down the remainder of the ones. Usually, we write down the subtraction that actually finds the remainder. Look carefully:

```
   0 6 1
4 )2 4 7
     - 4
       3
```

When dividing the ones, 4 goes into 7 one time. Multiply 1 × 4 = 4, write that four under the 7, and subract. This finds us the remainder of 3.

Check: 4 × 61 + 3 = 247

```
   0 4 0 2
4 )1 6 0 9
       - 8
         1
```

When dividing the ones, 4 goes into 9 two times. Multiply 2 × 4 = 8, write that eight under the 9, and subract. This finds us the remainder of 1.

Check: $4 \times 402 + 1 = 1{,}609$

Here are some example problems. Now, students check the answer by multiplying the divisor times the quotient, and then adding the remainder.

(a) $3\overline{)128}$

(b) $3\overline{)95}$

(c) $6\overline{)4267}$

(d) $4\overline{)2845}$

Step 3: A remainder in the tens

In this step, practice for the first time all the basic steps of long division algorithm: divide, multiply & subtract, drop down the next digit. We use two-digit numbers to keep it simple. Multiply & subtract has to do with finding the *remainder*, and after finding a remainder, we combine that with the next unit we are getting ready to divide (dropping down the digit).

An example:

---

1. Divide.

```
   t o
   2
2 )5 8
```

Two goes into 5 two times, or 5 tens ÷ 2 = 2 whole tens — but there is a remainder!

---

2. Multiply & subtract.

```
   t o
   2
2 )5 8
 -4
  1
```

To find it, multiply $2 \times 2 = 4$, write that 4 under the five, and subtract to find the remainder of 1 ten.

---

3. Drop down the next digit.

```
   t o
   2 9
2 )5 8
 -4
  1 8
```

Next, drop down the 8 of the ones next to the leftover 1 ten. You combine the remainder ten with 8 ones, and get 18.

---

1. Divide.

```
   t o
   2 9
2 )5 8
 -4
  1 8
```

Divide 2 into 18. Place 9 into the quotient.

---

2. Multiply & subtract.

```
   t o
   2 9
2 ) 5 8
  - 4
    1 8
  - 1 8
      0
```

Multiply $9 \times 2 = 18$, write that 18 under the 18, and subtract.

---

3. Drop down the next digit.

```
   t o
   2 9
2 ) 5 8
  - 4
    1 8
  - 1 8
      0
```

The division is over since there are no more digits in the dividend. The quotient is 29.

Step 4: A remainder in any of the place values

After the previous step has been mastered, students then practice long division with three- and four-digit numbers where they will have to go through the basic steps several times.

---

1. Divide.

```
   t o
   1
2 )2 7 8
```

Two goes into 2 one time, or 2 hundreds ÷ 2 = 1 hundred.

---

2. Multiply & subtract.

```
   t o
   1
2 )2 7 8
  -2
   0
```

Multiply 1 × 2 = 2, write that 2 under the two, and subtract to find the remainder of zero.

---

3. Drop down the next digit.

```
   t o
   1 8
2 )2 7 8
  -2 ↓
   0 7
```

Next, drop down the 7 of the tens next to the zero.

---

1. Divide.

```
   t o
   1 3
2 )2 7 8
  -2
   0 7
```

Divide 2 into 7. Place 3 into the quotient.

---

2. Multiply & subtract.

```
   t o
   1 3
2 ) 2 7 8
   -2
    0 7
   - 6
      1
```

Multiply 3 × 2 = 6, write that 6 under the 7, and subtract to find the remainder of 1 ten.

---

3. Drop down the next digit.

```
   t o
   1 3
2 ) 2 7 8
   -2
    0 7
   - 6
      1 8
```

Next, drop down the 8 of the ones next to the 1 leftover ten.

---

1. Divide.

```
    t o
    1 3 9
2 ) 2 7 8
   -2
    0 7
   - 6
      1 8
```

Divide 2 into 18. Place 9 into the quotient.

---

2. Multiply & subtract.

```
    t o
    1 3 9
2 ) 2 7 8
   -2
    0 7
   - 6
      1 8
    - 1 8
        0
```

Multiply 9 × 2 = 18, write that 18 under the 18, and subtract to find the remainder of zero.

---

3. Drop down the next digit.

```
    t o
    1 3 9
2 ) 2 7 8
   -2
    0 7
   - 6
      1 8
    - 1 8
        0
```

Some Exercises

Question Number 1

12 + 23 – 34 =

A. 1

B. 27

C. 38

D. 49

E. 50

F. 61

Question Number 2

45 – 56 + 67 =

A. 11

B. 56

C. 72

D. 83

E. 94

F. 05

Question Number 3

78 + 89 – 90 =

A. 16

B. 2

C. 77

D. 83

E. 94

F. 05

Question Number 4

09 – 98 + 87 =

A. 50

B. 61

C. 7

D. 2

E. 38

F. 49

Question Number 5

76 + 65 – 54 =

A. 94

B. 05

C. 16

D. 2

E. 87

F. 83

Question Number 6

43 - 32 + 21 =

A. 38

B. 49

C. 50

D. 61

E. 7

F. 32

Answers

1. c 2. b 3. a 4. d 5. e 6. f

Calculate % mentally

Percentage means out of 100, so 1% means 1 out of 100 and 50% means 50 out of 100. We can use this to help us calculate simple percentages of numbers. The rules are as follows:

1. To calculate 50% of a number you halve it. e.g. 50% of 234 = 117.
2. To calculate 25% of a number you halve it and then halve it again. This is because 25% is the same as 1/4. e.g. 25% of 64 = 16, because half of 64 is 32 and half of 32 is 16.
3. To calculate 75% you work out 50% then halve it to get 25% and then add the two answers together. e.g. 75% of 48 is 36.

   50% of 48 = 24
   25% of 48 = 12
   so 75% of 48 = 36
4. To calculate 10% of a number you divide the number by 10, because 10% is the same as 1/10. You can then multiply the answer to get 30%, 70%, 90% etc. e.g. 10% of 70 = 70 divided by 10 = 7, so 30% = 7 x 3 = 21 i.e.10% x3

   70% = 7 x 7 = 49 i.e.10% x7
5. To calculate 1% you divide by 100 because 1% = 1/100. You can use this answer to calculate 7%, 13%, 27% etc.

   e.g. 1% of 300 = 3, so 13% of 300 = 13 x 3 (13 x 1%) = 39.

Interesting Facts

- The word 'MATHEMATICS' comes from the Greek μαθημα (máthema), which means 'science, knowledge, or learning', μαθηματικόζ (mathematikós) means 'fond of learning'.
- The word 'FRACTION' derives from the Latin 'fractio - to break'.
- GEOMETRY(Ancient Greek: ψεωμετπια; geo = earth, metria = measure) is a part of mathematics.
- 'ALGEBRA' comes Arabic word (al-jabr, literally, restoration)
- There are just four numbers (after 1), which are the sums of the cubes of their digits:

  153 = 1^3 + 5^3 + 3^3

  370 = 3^3 + 7^3 + 0^3

  371 = 3^3 + 7^3 + 1^3

  407 = 4^3 + 0^3 + 7^3
- 111,111,111 multiplied by 111,111,111 equals 12,345,678,987,654,321.
- Among all shapes with the same area, circle has the shortest perimeter.
- For every object there is a distance at which it looks its best.
- The Five Most Important Numbers in Mathematics in One Equation:

  e^i*pi + 1 = 0

Mental Maths to Impress Friends

Math Magic/TricksTrick 1: Number below 10

Step1: Think of a number below 10.

Step2: Double the number you have thought.

Step3: Add 6 to the result.

Step4: Half the answer, that is divide it by 2.

Step5: Take away the number you have thought from the answer, that is, subtract the answer from the number you have thought. Answer: 3

Trick 2: Any Number

Step1: Think of any number.

Step2: Subtract the number you have thought with 1.

Step3: Multiply the result with 3.

Step4: Add 12 to the result.

Step5: Divide the answer by 3.

Step6: Add 5 to the answer.

Step7: Take away the number you have thought from the answer, that is, subtract the answer from the number you have thought. Answer: 8

Trick 3: Any Number

Step1: Think of any number.

Step2: Multiply the number you have thought with 3.

Step3: Add 45 with the result.

Step4: Double the result.

Step5: Divide the answer by 6.

Step6: Take away the number you have thought from the answer, that is, subtract the answer from the number you have thought. Answer: 15

Trick 4: Same 3 Digit Number

Step1: Think of any 3 digit number, but each of the digits must be the same as. Ex: 333, 666.

Step2: Add up the digits.

Step3: Divide the 3 digit number with the digits added up. Answer: 37

Trick 5: 2 Single Digit Numbers

Step1: Think of 2 single digit numbers.

Step2: Take any one of the number among them and double it.

Step3: Add 5 with the result.

Step4: Multiply the result with 5.

Step5: Add the second number to the answer.

Step6: Subtract the answer with 4.

Step7: Subtract the answer again with 21.

Answer: 2 Single Digit Numbers.

Trick 6: 1, 2, 4, 5, 7, 8

Step1: Choose a number from 1 to 6.

Step2: Multiply the number with 9.

Step3: Multiply the result with 111.

Step4: Multiply the result by 1001.

Step5: Divide the answer by 7.

Answer: All the above numbers will be present.

Trick 7: 1089

Step1: Think of a 3 digit number.

Step2: Arrange the number in descending order.

Step3: Reverse the number and subtract it with the result.

Step4: Remember it and reverse the answer mentally.

Step5: Add it with the result, you have got.

Answer: 1089

Trick 8: x7x11x13

Step1: Think of a 3 digit number.

Step2: Multiply it with x7x11x13.

Ex. Number: 456, Answer: 456456

Trick 9: x3x7x13x37

Step1: Think of a 2 digit number.

Step2: Multiply it with x3x7x13x37.

Ex. Number: 45, Answer: 454545

Trick 10: 9091

Step1: Think of a 5 digit number.

Step2: Multiply it with 11.

Step3: Multiply it with 9091.

Ex. Number: 12345, Answer: 1234512345

To the power of 10 = ?

Values	Zero's	Names
10^{0}	0	One
10^{1}	1	Ten
10^{2}	2	Hundred
10^{3}	3	Thousand
10^{4}	4	Myriad
10^{6}	6	Million
10^{9}	9	Billion
10^{12}	12	Trillion
10^{15}	15	Quadrillion
10^{18}	18	Quintillion
10^{21}	21	Sextillion
10^{24}	24	Septillion
10^{27}	27	Octillion
10^{30}	30	Nonillion
10^{33}	33	Decillion
10^{36}	36	Undecillion
10^{39}	39	Duodecillion
10^{42}	42	Tredecillion
10^{45}	45	Quattuordecillion
10^{48}	48	Quindecillion
10^{51}	51	Sexdecillion
10^{54}	54	Septdecillion / Septendecillion
10^{57}	57	Octodecillion

Values	Zero's	Names
10^{60}	60	Nondecillion / Novemdecillion
10^{63}	63	Vigintillion
10^{66}	66	Unvigintillion
10^{69}	69	Duovigintillion
10^{72}	72	Trevigintillion
10^{75}	75	Quattuorvigintillion
10^{78}	78	Quinvigintillion
10^{81}	81	Sexvigintillion
10^{84}	84	Septenvigintillion
10^{87}	87	Octovigintillion
10^{90}	90	Novemvigintillionn
10^{93}	93	Trigintillion
10^{96}	96	Untrigintillion
10^{99}	99	Duotrigintillion
10^{100}	100	Googol
10^{102}	102	Trestrigintillion
10^{120}	120	Novemtrigintillion
10^{123}	123	Quadragintillion
10^{138}	138	Quinto-Quadragintillion
10^{153}	153	Quinquagintillion
10^{180}	180	Novemquinquagintillion
10^{183}	183	Sexagintillion
10^{213}	213	Septuagintillion
10^{240}	240	Novemseptuagintillion
10^{243}	243	Octogintillion
10^{261}	261	Sexoctogintillion

Values	Zero's	Names	
10^{273}	273	Nonagintillion	
10^{300}	300	Novemnonagintillion	
10^{303}	303	Centillion	
10^{309}	309	Duocentillion	
10^{312}	312	Trescentillion	
10^{351}	351	Centumsedecillion	10^{366}
366Primo-Vigesimo-Centillion		10^{402} 402	
Trestrigintacentillion		10^{603} 603	
Ducentillion			
10^{624}	624	Septenducentillion	10^{903}
903 Trecentillion			
10^{2421}	2421	Sexoctingentillion	
10^{3003}	3003	Millillion	
$10^{3000003}$	3000003	Milli-Millillion	

Did you know?

The implicit curve equation (x2+y2-1)3-x2y3=0 produces the heart shape.

The term Googol (10100, ie, 10 followed by 100 zeros) was invented by a 9-year old boy Milton Sirotta.

A Palindrome Number is a number that reads the same backwards and forward, e.g. 13431.

A dollar can be made into small change in 293 ways.

You can remember the value of Pi (3.1415926) by counting each word's letters in 'May I have a large container of coffee?'

Multiplication and succession:

$1 \times 8 + 1 = 9$

$12 \times 8 + 2 = 98$

$123 \times 8 + 3 = 987$

142857 is a cyclic number, i.e., its digits are rotated around when multiplied by any number from 1 to 6. Like this:

142857 × 1 = 142857

142857 × 5 = 7 14285

142857 × 4 = 57 1428

142857 × 6 = 857 142

142857 × 2 = 2857 14

142857 × 3 = 42857 1

1089 multiplied by 9 gives an exact reverse: 9801.

From 0 to 1000, the letter 'A' only appears in 1000 ('one thousand').

2 is called the 'oddest' Even-Prime number. 2 is a unique Even-Prime because while all Evens are divisible by 2, any number apart from 2 that is divisible by 2, is not a Prime.

$1 \times 9 + 2 = 11$

$12 \times 9 + 3 = 111$

$123 \times 9 + 4 = 1111$

... and so on

40 when written 'forty' is the only number with letters in alphabetical order, while 'one' is the only one with letters in reverse order.

1 googol = 10100

1 googolplex = 10googol = 1010100

(The 'Google' website name was inspired by 'Googol'.)

$111\,111\,111 \times 111\,111\,111$

=

12345678 9 87654321

Pi (3.14159...) is a number that cannot be written as a fraction. Sciensational.com

The opposite sides of a dice cube always add up to seven.

21978 when multiplied by 4 is the same number with digits in reverse order:

$21978 \times 4 = 87912$

Sciensational.com

If you add up the numbers 1-100 consecutively (1+2+3+4+5...) the total is 5050. Sciensational.com

The billionth digit of Pi is 9. Sciensational.com

1 and 2 are the only numbers where they are the values of the numbers of factors they have. Sciensational.com

2 and 5 are the only prime numbers that end in 2 or 5.

The largest known prime number (so far) is 12,978,189 digits long. Sciensational.com

The digits to the right of the Pi's (3.141...) decimal point can keep going forever, and there is no pattern to these digits at all.

Pi = 3.14159 26535 89793 23846 26433 83279 50288 41971 69399 37510 58209 74944 59230 78164 06286 20899 86280 34825 34211 70679 82148 08651 32823 ...

A sphere has two sides. However, there are one-sided surfaces.

There are shapes of constant width other than the circle. One can even drill square holes.

There are just five regular polyhedra.

In a group of 23 people, at least two have the same birthday with the probability greater than 1/2.

Everything you can do with a ruler and a compass you can do with the compass alone.

Among all shapes with the same perimeter a circle has the largest area.

There are curves that fill a plane without holes.

Much as with people, there are irrational, perfect, complex numbers.

As in philosophy, there are transcendental numbers.

As in the art, there are imaginary and surreal numbers.

A straight line has dimension 1, a plane - 2. Fractals have mostly fractional dimension.

You are wrong if you think Mathematics is not fun.

Mathematics studies neighbourhoods, groups and free groups, rings, ideals, holes, poles and removable poles, trees, growth ...

Mathematics also studies models, shapes, curves, cardinals, similarity, consistency, completeness, space ...

Among objects of mathematical study are heredity, continuity, jumps, infinity, infinitesimals, paradoxes...

Last but not the least, Mathematics studies stability, projections and values, values are often absolute, but may also be extreme, local or global.

Trigonometry aside, Mathematics comprises fields like Game Theory, Braids Theory, Knot Theory and more.

One is morally obligated not to do anything impossible.

Some numbers are square, yet others are triangular.

The next sentence is true, but you must not believe it

The previous sentence was false.

12+3-4+5+67+8+9=100 and there exists at least one other representation of 100 with 9 digits in the right order and math operations in between.

One can cut a pie into 8 pieces with three movements.

Program=Algorithms+Data Structures

There is something the dead eat, but if the living eat it, they die.

A clock never showing right time might be preferable to the one showing right time twice a day.

Among all shapes with the same area, the circle has the shortest perimeter.

Math Jokes

- What do mathematicians eat on Halloween? Pumpkin Pi.
- Why did the math book look so sad? Because it had so many problems.
- A circle is just a round straight line with a hole in the middle.
- Decimals have a point.
- Why do plants hate math? Because it gives them square roots.
- Why did the boy eat his math homework? Because the teacher told him it was a piece of cake.
- Have you heard the latest statistics joke? Probably.
- What did the acorn say when it grew up? Geometry.
- What do you call an empty parrot cage? Polygon.
- Cakes are round, but Pi are square.
- How can you make time fly? Throw a clock out the window!
- Without geometry, life is pointless.

Math Limericks

1. An algebra teacher named Drew
   Tried to find the clue.
   He found it between
   1/4 and 14,
   But couldn't get closer. Can you?
2. There was an old man who said, 'Do
   Tell me how I should add two and two.
   I think more and more
   That it makes about four —
   But I fear that is almost too few.'
3. There was a young lady called Kate,
   Whose maths was right up-to-date.
   She said, 'It is fun
   When three 3's are one —
   Which they are with module 8.'
4. Little Jack Horner sat in a corner,
   Trying to evaluate.
   He disclaimed rule of thumb,
   Found an infinite sum,
   And exclaimed 'It's REAL, and i.'

5. A mathematician named Ray
   Says extraction of roots is child's play.
   You don't need equations
   Or long calculations;
   Just hot water to run on the tray.

6. Said Mrs. Isosceles Tri,
   'That I'm sharp I've no wish to deny;
   But I do not dare
   To be perfectly square —
   I'm sure if I did I should die!'

7. An arithmetic teacher named Jones
   Was reduced by the new math to groans,
   And shortly expired.
   Since he has not retired,
   He now serves as Napier's Bones.

8. A mathematician confided
   That a Moebius band is one-sided.
   And you'll get quite a laugh
   If you cut one in half,
   For it stays in one piece when divided.

9. A graduate student at Trinity
   Computed the square of infinity.

But it gave him the fidgets
To put down the digits,
So he dropped math and took up divinity.

10. A mathematician from Boole,
Used to mispronounce words like a fool.
He spoke of 'stastistics',
And 'intragel' ballistics,
'Yuler' circles and 'Hospital's' rule.

11. There was a young student from Rye,
Who worked out the value of.
'It happens,' said he,
'That it's just over 3,
Though I'd rather you don't ask me why.'

12. There was a young student from Crewe
Who learned how to count in base 2.
His sums were all done
With 0 and 1,
And he found it much simpler to do.

13. There was a young fellow called Dan,
Who knew all about sin, cos and tan.
He talked rather big

Of his knowledge of trig —
He did seem a clever young man.

14. A modern young lady called Rita,
Buys ribbons and cloth by the metre.
She gets bacon and ham
Weighed out by the gram,
And orders her milk by the litre.

15. There was a maths student called Hector,
Who couldn't tell scalar from vector.
'I'm quite at a loss
To tell a dot from a cross —
I ought not to work in this sector.'

16. If inside a circle, a line
Hits the center and goes from spine to spine
And the line's length is 'd',
The circumference will be
d times 3.14159.

17. A Dozen, a Gross and a Score,
plus three times the square root of four,
divided by seven,
plus five times eleven,
equals nine squared and not a bit more.

18. 'Tis a favorite project of mine
A new value of pi to assign.
I would fix it at 3
For it's simpler, you see,
Than 3 point 1 4 1 5 9.

19. There was a young man named Floogle,
Who tried to count up to a googol.
But it took such a long time
That one day he cried, 'I'm
Now known as the Old Man Floogle.'

20. There once was a woman from Dundee,
Whose age had last digit three.
If her whole age reversed
Is the square of the first (digit),
Then what must the woman's age be?

21. A Pi Lymeric
There once was a number Pi
Very special like e and phi
Circumference to d
Is the ratio for me
And it's not a multiple of i

22. There was a Young Lady from Bath,
In love she was—and deeply—with Math;
She married a Fraction,

But died of Subtraction,
That algebraic Young Lady from Bath.

23. The system which we use is decimal,
But the ancient Mayans used vigesimal.
Base TWENTY, not ten
Was what suited them then.
Tell that to your friends and impress 'em all!

24. The 'long hundred' once signified plenty:
It meant more than the standard 'short' century
Base TWELVE was the count
Which increased the amount;
TWELVE times ten gives one hundred and twenty

25. Integral z-squared dz
From 1 to the cube root of 3
Times the cosine
Of three pi over 9
Equals log of the cube root of 'e'.

26. When you cut Apollonius' cone
There's a circle, but it's not alone.
A parabola, new,
A hyperbola, too,
And a perfect ellipse will be shown.

Types of Graphs

Pie Graph

A pie graph, also known as a pie chart, is a type of graph commonly used in conjunction with percentages. A large circle is divided into sections depending on those percentages and each section represents part of the whole. In a pie chart, the arc length of each separate sector is meant to be proportional to the percentage it's supposed to represent. The first pie chart was created in 1801 by William Playfair.

Bar Graph

A bar graph, or bar chart, is used to represent values in relation to other values. They're often used to compare data taken over long periods of time, but they're most often used on very small sets of data. These graphs can be horizontal or vertical. If it's horizontal, the 'categories' for what the actual data represents is across the bottom and at the side, horizontally, are numbers that represent the actual data.

Line Graph

A line graph is slightly harder to define. They are meant to compare two separate variables and these variables are both plotted on an axis. In the end, you get a graph with lines that go from a fixed point across a chart, going up and down, in relation to data.

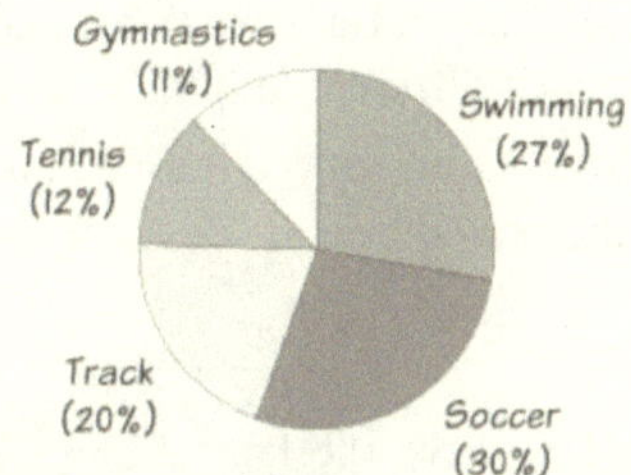

A pie chart is a circular chart divided into sectors, each sector shows the relative size of each value.

Line Graph: A graph that shows information that is connected in some way (such as change over time).

You are learning math facts, and each day you do a short test to see how good you are. These are the results:

Table: Facts I got Correct

Day 1	Day 2	Day 3	Day 4
3	4	12	15

And here is the same data as a Line Graph:

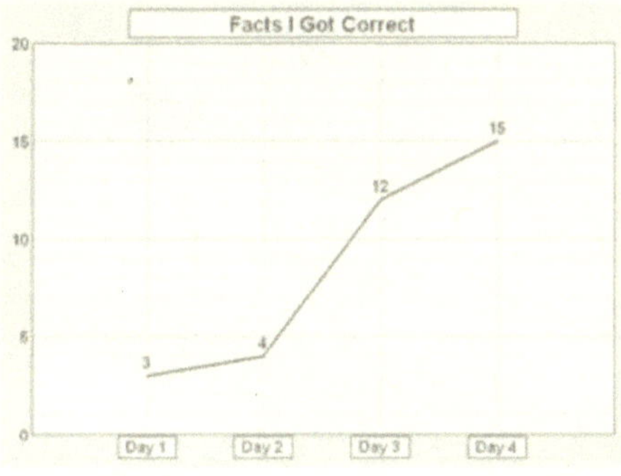

A **Bar Graph** (also called Bar Chart) is a graphical display of data using bars of different heights.

Imagine you just did a survey of your friends to find which kind of movie they liked best.

Here are the results:

Table: Favourite Type of Movie

Comedy	Action	Romance	Drama	SciFi
4	5	6	1	4

You could show that on a bar graph like this:

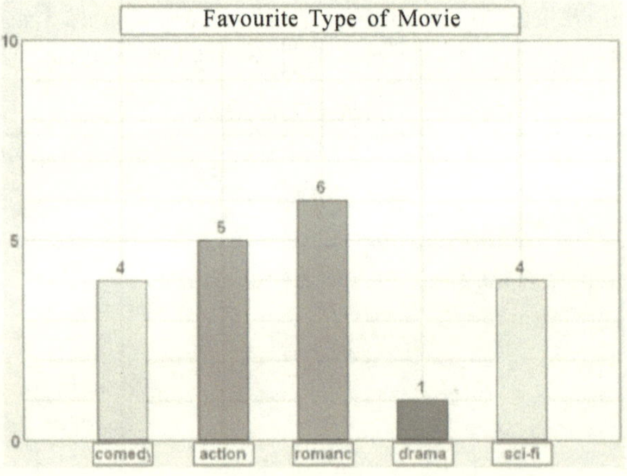

www.ingramcontent.com/pod-product-compliance
Lightning Source LLC
La Vergne TN
LVHW050934080826
845145LV00004B/1261

* 9 7 8 8 1 2 9 1 2 3 8 2 4 *